Tenerife Temptation

L.M. Evans

Tenerife Temptation

Tenerife Temptation

A Holiday Romance

By
L.M. Evans

L.M. Evans

Tenerife Temptation

Copyright

Copyright © 2019 by L.M. Evans

All rights reserved. No part of this publication may be reproduced, distributed, or transmitted in any form or by any means, including photocopying, recording, or other electronic or mechanical methods, without the prior written permission of the author, except in the case of brief quotations embodied in critical reviews and certain other non-commercial uses permitted by copyright law.

This is a work of fiction. Names, characters, businesses, places, events, and incidents are either the products of the author's imagination or used in a fictitious manner. Any resemblance to actual persons, living or dead, or actual events is purely coincidental.

The authors are not affiliated with any brands, songs or musicians or artists mentioned in this book.

Edited by Maria Lazarou ~ Obsessed by Books Designs
Formatter: Maria Lazarou ~ Obsessed by Books Designs
Cover Designer: Maria Lazarou ~ Obsessed by Books Designs

L.M. Evans

Tenerife Temptation

Contents

COPYRIGHT V

CONTENTS VII

DEDICATION IX

ACKNOWLEDGEMENTS XI

BLURB XIII

CHAPTER ONE .... - 1 -

CHAPTER TWO .... - 6 -

CHAPTER THREE .... - 11 -

CHAPTER FOUR .... - 17 -

CHAPTER FIVE .... - 20 -

CHAPTERS SIX .... - 25 -

CHAPTER SEVEN .... - 31 -

CHAPTER EIGHT .... - 39 -

CHAPTER NINE .... - 46 -

CHAPTER TEN .... - 53 -

CHAPTER ELEVEN .... - 60 -

CHAPTER TWELVE .... - 67 -

CHAPTER THIRTEEN .... - 75 -

CHAPTER FOURTEEN .... - 79 -

CHAPTER FIFTEEN .... - 87 -

CHAPTER SIXTEEN .... - 96 -

CHAPTER SEVENTEEN .... - 103 -

CHAPTER EIGHTEEN .... - 110 -

CHAPTER NINETEEN .... - 116 -

AUTHOR BIO..	- 127 -
CONTACT AUTHOR	- 129 -

Tenerife Temptation

Dedication

This book is dedicated to my nan
Jeanette.
You are my guardian angel always
shining bright when I need you.
Love you always

xx

L.M. Evans

x

Tenerife Temptation

Acknowledgements

To my husband and children, I love you all. Thank you for letting me follow a dream and to do what I thought was never possible.

Thank you to my parents for making sure I kept up with my schoolwork when I was younger. To my sisters, family, and friends for supporting and believing in me, I love you all.

Being an indie author is scary there can be dark sides but also loads of good. If you are lucky enough to surround yourself with amazing people, then you are truly blessed. I have made so many friends along the way since I began this journey. To those who started this crazy train with me and those who have hopped on board since I couldn't do this without your support it means so much. So, I want to say thank you to Debbie Williams, Mia Hudson, Diane Lewis, Christine Lewis, Beth Jones, Nicola Yates, M. A. Foster, Sienna Grant, Scarlet Le Clair, Emma Lloyd, Leanne Colvin, Keira Garbett,

I also want to say a massive thank you to my editor and Cover Designer Maria I don't know where I would be without you.

L.M. Evans

Lastly, I want to say a massive thank you to all the bloggers who helped spread the word about my work.

Tenerife Temptation

Blurb

Taylor

Summer is finally here, and after two years of working my ass off at college, I am finally a qualified support teacher. A girls' holiday in Tenerife with my best friend is exactly what I need.

I'm not interested in romance; I just want to kick back and relax.

However, life is full of surprises, and love walks in when I'm least expecting it.

Brooklyn

Keeping secrets from everyone is hard work, especially when the one person who is meant to have my back does nothing but criticise me.

A lads' holiday is exactly what I need to chill out and get the creative juices flowing again.

What I don't expect is for inspiration to smack me square in the face.

Tenerife Temptation

There is never a time or place for true love.
It happens accidentally, in a heartbeat,
in a single flashing, throbbing moment."

Unknown

L.M. Evans

Tenerife Temptation

Chapter One

The airport is busy, people everywhere. Everyone going to various check-in desks, booking in to board their planes. Queues were forming with people excited about their upcoming travels.

Me and my best friend Stacee, booked a week in the sun to celebrate finishing college. We started planning our trip before we started our last year.

"T, I can't believe we are finally done with college after three years, it's crazy." Stacee says as we wait in line to check in for our flight to Tenerife.

"I know, those years have flown by and now here we are jetting off on holiday. All the studying and hard work was worth it and now we get to relax in the sun." I say just as we get to the front of the line to check-in.

"Passports and tickets please." The woman wearing a white blouse with an orange scarf and an easy jet label, behind the desk asks.

We take twenty minutes to get checked in. Once we are done, we make our way through to the departure lounge where the duty-free shops are; we had to be at the airport two hours before our flight. We have just over an hour left before we board. So, we head over to the bar for a few drinks while we wait. We place our order and then find somewhere to sit. I pick up my bottle of WKD in a toast.

"Here is to sun, sea and sangria."

"No, here is to sun, sea and sexy men," Stacee adds, lifting her bottle of Bud as we clink our drinks.

Maybe she's right, I've been single for nearly a year and a holiday fling is just what I need to get back on the horse.

The hour seems to go really fast, by the time we're due to board the plane, we both had drunk a few bottles. Boarding seemed to take forever, calling out boarding numbers, checking the tickets and our passports. We found our seats and stowed our hand luggage in the overhead compartments "Excuse ladies, I think that's my seat by the window." A tall guy says, stopping by our seats.

I glance up and my eyes meet a pair of the most perfect emerald green eyes staring back at me. He looks like a model with slicked back, dark brown hair, wearing a light blue shirt, that's slightly open, revealing some of his chest. Stacee elbows me in the side, bringing me out of my daze.

"Sorry," I say, as we both stood up to let the mysterious hunk climb into his seat.

We sit back down and put our seatbelts on ready for take-off. The cabin crew go through all the safety and emergency procedures before sitting down themselves.

Stacee closes her eyes, she's always been nervous about flying.

"Is she okay?" Mr. mysterious leans in to whisper.

Glancing over at Stacee, I turn to reply, "Yeah she just hates the taking off and landing part." I explain.

"I'm Jake, by the way," Mr. mystery man says introducing himself.

"Nice to meet you Jake. I'm Taylor and that's Stacee."

The plane starts taxing down the runway slowly and turns around before coming to a stop.

"Taylor, give me a nudge when we can take the belts off will you." Stacee asks and then goes silent.

The pilot announces we are just about to take off and how long the flight will be, as well as the time we are due to arrive. The cabin lights dim as the aircraft shoots forward like a rocket. The force of the plane moving so fast makes me grip the arm rests, hard. I'm no way scared of flying but the take-off does make me slightly nervous.

"Hey Taylor." Jake says. I turn to face him.

"Yeah."

His eyes are mesmerising. He scoots closer, never once moving his eye from mine.

"Your eyes are so hypnotizing." I say and he chuckles.

"Thanks, that's one I've never heard before." He replies as the captain announces we can take our seatbelts off.

I suddenly have the urge to use the toilet, so I turn away from Jake to hide my embarrassment and nudge Stacee to let her know we are in the air.

"I need the bathroom," I tell her, so I stand up and squeeze past.

Moving up the plane, I locate the toilet. There is one person in front of me so I wait my turn, I can't believe what I just said to Jake, he must think I'm some sort of nutter.

When I get back to my seat Jake is gone and Stacee has her head in her book.

"Hey T, what took you so long, I thought you got sucked in to the toilet." She jokes.

"Hardy har so not funny." I reply sarcastically and sit back down. "Where did Jake go?" I ask, motioning to the empty window seat.

"Oh, Mr Dreamy? He went to see if he could find his friends, he's on a stag weekend. Him and another lad Shane, are not sitting with the rest of the them."

"Ah, so did you have a nice chat while I went to hide my embarrassment?"

"Well you shouldn't have been making goo, goo eyes at him, then he wouldn't have hypnotized you" Stacee teases. Just as Jake comes back.

We spent the rest of the two-hour flight talking to Jake. Turns out he's on a stag holiday for a week, with nine other lads.

Finally landing at Sofia Airport in Tenerife; it is nearly nine o'clock at night. We spend the next forty-five minutes waiting to get our suitcases and finding the tour representative, who shows us to our coach.

The ride to the hotel was quiet but, on the inside, I was excited for us to get to our hotel.

Chapter Two

The sounds of people talking loudly wakes me up, Stacee is still out cold. Pushing the blankets off me, I swing my feet over the edge, stroll over to the open balcony door and walk out. Glancing down, I take in my surroundings. I notice that there is massive pool below and just off to the side of it is a small kiddies one. Surrounding the pools are quite a few sun loungers, some have a few big, beach towels on them.

The voices that woke me up become clearer, they were coming from two hotel male employees, wearing white polo shirts with the hotel name on and matching shorts. They seemed to be laughing about something, while walking from the hut on the far side of the pool.

"You will get used to being woken up in the mornings if you leave your balcony door open at night." A voice says from the balcony next door making me jump.

"Jesus." I say clutching my chest, my heart is racing.

"Sorry, I didn't mean to scare you. We arrived in two nights ago and we leave our balcony door open at night because it gets so stuffy." A head sticks out over the balcony wall. "My name is Suzy by the way." She smiles, so I smile back.

"No worries, I'm Taylor. I'm here with my best friend Stacee, she's still asleep."

"Nice to meet you Taylor, how long you here for?"

"Only a week, we arrived late last night. What about you, are you here alone?"

"No, I'm here with my sister Brie, we are here for ten days. You should come tag along with us, we are going over to the Venture tomorrow night."

"What is the Venture?" I ask, puzzled.

"It's a big complex with shops, restaurants and nightclubs. We loved it we went there last night and Brie partied hard, so she's not going to surface until dinner time. So, I'm going to chill by the pool and work on my tan with a book," she explains.

"I think we'll probably do the same today. So, we may see you down there, I'm going to get changed and wake Stacee up." I explain and then walk back in the room. Stacee is sat up in bed with an amused look on her face.

"What's so funny?" I ask.

She motions for me to close the door to the balcony, so I do.

"Well aren't you a people magnet. First, Mr Handsome on the plane and now our next-door neighbour." She giggles.

"I can't help it if people like talking to me." I reply and poke my tongue out at her. "Come on, let's get changed and take our towels and put them on two sun loungers before we go have breakfast."

Fifteen minutes later, we are dressed in shorts and vest tops, with our bikinis underneath and our flip flops on our feet. We walk down to the restaurant with our bags and towels. Stopping by the pool on the way, we place our beach towels on two sun loungers, before heading to breakfast.

The smell of eggs, bacon, and warm pastries fills the air, the dining hall is split into two sections. The main part of it is massive, cream, marble floor tiles, white walls, and cream net curtains, that flow either side of the windows. Rows of white tables and chairs fill one side of the dining hall. The other side is filled with counters with various different items, one with all different cereals, another with cooked breakfast items. Bacon, tomatoes, mushrooms, beans, and fried bread. There is another counter to make toast, and another one to have fried eggs or pancakes. A different section has various pastries as well as one for hot or cold drinks. There's also one for different fruits.

"Wow can you believe this place, it's incredible," Stacee says from beside me.

"I know it's amazing. I think I'm going to have some cereal and fruit, then some toast later."

"Mmm, I fancy some pancakes and some fruit for breakfast."

Stacee says before walking off toward where those items are located, she joins the queue of people waiting to make their pancakes. I walk over to the area with all the cereals, and grab a bowl from the counter, I take a few steps decide on some coco pops. I pour some milk from the chiller at the end of the counter over my cereal, then walk over to the counter with all the fruit I grab an apple before finding a table to sit at. Finding one that is close to where all the breakfast items are located to make sure that Stacee will be able to find me. The table is already set with cutlery, so I take a seat and begin eating my breakfast.

"The guy who is making the pancakes is so cute," Stacee says as she pulls out the chair opposite me.

"Ah so that's what was keeping you, you were flirting with the hotel staff." I tease.

"I wasn't flirting… Okay, maybe just a little," she admits.

"We need to find out when the holiday reps are about and find out what excursions happening." I suggest.

"I overheard one of the other guests saying there is a meeting at ten in the hotel lobby, opposite the bar, so…" She pauses and presses the button on her phone to check the time.

"We have about thirty minutes to eat, in order to make it on time."

We both finish eating, after we went back for some toast and juice, then make our way to the hotel lobby. Taking a seat on the big cream sofa in the corner, we wait with a few other guests. We don't have to wait long before two male holiday reps wearing blue polo shirts and cream trousers, holding a shoulder and a laptop bag, walk over to a table. The tall guy with blond hair who is holding the laptop bag, sits down and pulls the laptop out of his bag. While the slightly shorter one with brown hair, who was carrying a black shoulder bag, takes a seat beside the blond guy.

"Good morning everyone, welcome to the Carlton hotel and Spa in Tenerife. My name is Jordan and this is my colleague Ross. We will be your hotel representatives while you're staying at the hotel. Now we can't always be on site as we are reps at a number of hotels, so if you have any questions when we aren't available there is a list of numbers on the wall behind the table as you enter the dining area." Jordan explains.

Ross stands up with some leaflets in his hand.

"We have a number of excursions over the coming days, so let us tell you what we have to offer, should you wish to go travelling around the island. Now you don't have to sign up but we do recommend you take advantage of the offers we have."

He goes on to explain the various excursions that they have on various days. We decide to only go to the Aqua park one and spend the rest of the time exploring the Island on our own. When we weren't topping up our tan by the side of the pool, that is.

Chapter Three

As the sun rises, so does the temperature, it's boiling by midday. I can't take it much longer; I need to cool down.

Sitting up, I swing my feet over the edge of the sun lounger, and notice that Stacee has her eyes closed. Taking off my sunglasses, I stand up and walk over to the pool, before jumping in to cool down. The water is slightly warm but feels good on my skin after baking in the sun for a few hours after breakfast. There are a quite a few people in the pool. As well as some surrounding the pool area on sun loungers. I swim back and forth a few times, before stopping down at the deeper end of the pool and lean on the side.

"There you are, do you fancy coming to the sauna on the roof for half hour?" Stacee asks while crouching down in front of me.

"Are you crazy? It's nearly thirty degrees right now and you want to go into a sauna that is between seventy and ninety degrees in there…"

She cuts me off.

"So that's a no then?"

"Damn straight it's a no. I mad but I'm not that bloody mad, sorry you are on your own for the sauna. I'm going to dry off after a few more laps and have a cocktail, then read my book on my sun lounger."

"Okay no worries, I'll see you in an hour back in the room."

"Okay try not to overcook yourself" I shout teasingly.

She pokes her tongue out, then walks off.

Three hours later, I lost track of time while reading my book lounging by the pool. I quickly grab my bag and shove my book and sun cream in. Before placing my glasses on top of my head and slipping my flip flops on my feet. Leaning over, I pick up my beach towel from the back of the lounger and toss it over my shoulder, then quickly make my way up to our hotel room. Taking the key card out of my bag, I place it in the door lock to unlock it, it turns green and releases the lock. I take the key card out of the lock and push the door open, Stacee is on her bed making out with some guy.

"Oh shoot, I'm gonna…"

I don't finish my sentence but instead turn around and rush out of the room. I walk fast down to the hotel lobby and place my bag and towel on the sofas opposite the bar area, before walking up to the bar to get a drink.

"What can I get you to drink Miss?" The barman asks.

"Sex on the beach please." I tell him and he quickly mixes up my cocktail, then hands it back to me.

Walking back over to the sofa I take a seat; I can't believe what I just walked in on. I'm lost in thought about what I just witnessed, when something catches the corner of my eye. Turning my head, a guy with dark brown hair, wearing light blue shorts and a white tank top is standing there staring at me.

"Can I help you with something?"

His lips rise to a smile.

"Sorry you must think I'm some sort of weirdo just standing here staring. I wasn't sure it was you. I noticed you earlier by the pool, you were so engrossed in the book you were reading," he explains.

"Oh yes. I love to read, when I am really into a book, I can lose myself for hours."

"Would you mind me joining you?" he asks pointing to the space beside me.

I shake my head and motion for him to take a seat.

"Thanks, oh my name is Brooklyn by the way."

"I'm Taylor."

"What is the book about?" he asks, seemingly, genuinely interested.

Placing my drink on the floor, I dig into my bag and grab the book to show him.

"The book is a high school romance, the author Abbi Glines is one of my go to authors." I say as I hand him the book to have a look at.

He turns the book over and reads the back.

"Oh, I haven't read any of this author's work before, does she write other genres?" he asks, while a hands the book back to me.

"Yeah, she has a series called Existence which is paranormal, it is a bit darker than what I'm currently reading, but it's another good series. Do you read?"

"I do actually yeah, I like thrillers. So, are you here for long?" he asks changing the subject.

"Yeah, myself and Stacee, my best friend are here for a week, today is our first proper day here as we got in late last night. What about you?"

"We are here for two weeks this is our second week, I'm here with the lads for a holiday."

Just as he was about to say more, someone calls him

"Brooklyn, you ready.?"

A guy calls from the door near the exit. He turns to see who it is calling him and raises his finger telling him he be one minute.

"I better move, my friends are waiting for me, it was nice meeting you Taylor." he says as he stands.

"You too Brooklyn." I reply, then he walks off to catch up with his friends.

I finish the rest of my drink and slowly make my way back up to my hotel room, instead of unlocking the door, I decide to knock.

A few minutes later, the door opens.

"Oh my God T, I am so sorry you walked in on that earlier, he's gone now." Stacee explains.

I walk into the room, closing the door behind me.

"Look Stacee, I don't care if you want to hook up with some guy while we are on holiday but some warning would have been nice. Maybe a note on the door or something…."

"I know, I know, but we were only kissing. We hadn't long got back to the room before you walked in. I met him when I went up to the roof, he was on his own catching some sun in a tiny pair of speedos on a sun lounger…" She pauses as if she's reliving that moment.

"Stacee," I say clicking my fingers to snap her out of her day dream.

"Oh sorry, yeah he was on the sun lounger and I went to go in the sauna but it was shut. So I decided to stay and enjoy the view on the roof. Then we started talking and I asked him to rub some sun cream on my back, then we ended up back here. Oh my God T, he's so bloody ripped, those abs, those muscles. He's so yum."

"Stacee, oh my God, did you even get his name before you started drooling over his body?"

"Hell, yes I did. I got his number too" she grins like the Cheshire cat in Alice in wonderland.

"Well…?"

"His name is Raphael Valentino, he's twenty-three, originally from Rome in Italy, but he now lives in Manchester with his brother Giulio."

"Well I am going to jump in the shower and get ready to go to lunch."

"Okay, I had a shower when Raph left, so I'm going to change for dinner." Stacee adds before I go into the en suite.

Tenerife Temptation

Chapter Four

The dining room, is set up the same way as it was for breakfast, only difference now is that there are various delicacies for dinner. They have curries, rice, squid rings which were basically onion rings but with squid instead. As well as some traditional foods like wedges but with a Spanish twist. Chicken bites, pizza's, and Spanish sausage. I decide to have Spanish sausage with some wedges before walking over to grab a table. Just as I sit down, Stacee strolls over with her plate and places it on the table, before taking a seat opposite me.

"So, what should we do tonight?" I ask her, then take a bite of the sausage.

"Well, maybe we could go see what other nightlife the island have to offer." She replies, just as a group of four guys walk by, I recognise two of them.

One is Brooklyn and the other is the lad that was calling his name earlier, Brooklyn winks at me as he walks by. It doesn't go unnoticed by Stacee that my head is somewhere else.

"Who is the hunk that was eying you up as he walked passed just now?"

"He's just a guy that came over and started talking to me earlier when I was in the lobby." I reply, then place more food from my plate into my mouth.

She raises her eyebrows, "Oh really. So, I wasn't the only one having some fun today…?"

I cut her off after swallowing my food

"It wasn't like that, he saw me by the pool with my head in my Abbi Glines book and he just came over to ask me about it, he's…"

"Coming this way."

I turn around just as Brooklyn stops beside our table.

"Ladies, sorry for interrupting, I was wondering what you girls were up to after lunch?" he asks glancing between myself and Stacee.

"Well, we haven't really decided yet, I'm Stacee by the way and you are Brooklyn, right?"

"Nice to meet you Stacee," he says while holding his hand out towards her and she shakes it. "Well me and the guys are going over to Venture after lunch, we're going to the cocktail bar GiGi's before going to the nightclub Shake, Rattle n roll. Do you girls fancy coming with us?"

"Sure, we need to go back to our room first, so maybe you can meet us in the lobby in about twenty minutes?"

Brooklyn agrees then walks back over to his friends.

"Why do we need to go back to our room? I question after he's gone.

"We are going to change out of these dresses into skirts and very revealing tops, that guy is so freaking hot for you. You can't even see it."

I was about to reply when she held her hand up to stop me.

"No, you don't."

"I…"

"We are here to have fun and a good time, so we are joining those lads. I am telling you now, before the night is out you will be all over Brooklyn. Come on let's finish up and hurry back to our room to change, we can't keep Mr dream boat waiting," she smirks.

We quickly finish our food then head back to our room. There's no point in even trying to argue with Stacee, so I just follow her.

Chapter five

fifteen minutes later, we are both changed, Stacee into her short, blue denim skirt and sexy white top, that laces up the front. I decided to wear my black miniskirt and a red top like Stacee's.

"I still can't believe you convinced me to buy this, it looks slutty." I say as we walk from the lift to the lobby.

"Ooo look, loverboys jaw is on the floor." Stacee whispers as we approach where the guys are standing.

Glancing up at Brooklyn, our eyes meet and I smile.

"Hope we didn't keep you guys waiting long?" I say. Brooklyn walks toward us.

"Nah, we just got here. Let me introduce you to the guys, this is Cameron, Nathan, and Leo. Lads, this is Taylor and Stacee."

Each lad gives us a wave as Brooklyn introduces them. We follow them out of the hotel as they lead us to Venture.

"So Stacee, are you single?" Cameron asks flirtingly.

"Jesus Cam, buy the girl a drink before you drill her." Brooklyn teases. "You will have to excuse Cameron, Stacee, he doesn't think before he speaks…"

Brooklyn is cut off by Nathan.

"Yeah, he thinks with his dick not his head."

"Screw you both." Cameron shouts and walks ahead of everyone.

"Aww leave him alone. Hey Cameron." Stacee shouts, he stops and turns around. "Buy me a cocktail and show me your dance moves, then I might just tell you if I'm single or not." She teases, walks up to him and hooks her arm through his.

I shake my head and walk behind her and Cameron. It doesn't take us long before we get to Venture. It's like a massive complex, full with shops, bars, and restaurants.

"Wow this place is huge, do you guys come here every day?" I ask, while taking in my surroundings.

"We found this place on the second day here, since then we come here every day after lunch, its comes alive at night." Brooklyn explains.

"Come on let's go get our sesh on." Nathan says.

We all follow him to the cocktail bar.

"These are on me," Cameron shouts as we approach the bar.

"What can I get for you?" the barman asks.

"Six, Sex On The Beach cocktails and twelve shots of Sourz. Please," he replies.

"Bloody hell man, you planning on going back to the hotel early? You be rat-arsed before we get to the nightclub at this rate." Leo who has been quiet until now chimes in.

"Nah I be fine, here you go ladies," he says handing us two shots each. "Lads come and grab your shots."

"To sun, sea and Tenerife." Cameron adds.

We down both shots, one straight after the other, then we pick up our cocktails from the bar counter and grab a table.

As the day turns into night Cameron is getting more drunk and getting really handsy with Stacee. He keeps trying to touch her arms and neck, at one point he tries to kiss her on there. I can see its annoying the hell out of her and the rest of the guys can see it too. As three guys walk into the bar, Stacee jumps up, climbs over Cameron, who is wobbling side to side and runs over to one guy.

"Raph baby," she shouts.

The guy turns around and she runs straight at him, he picks her up, kisses her like she belongs to him, and squeezes her arse.

One of his friends taps him in the shoulder and he places Stacee back on the ground, but still holds her tight against his side. His arousal is not hard to miss, he is clearly in to her as much as she is him. He says something to his friends before they both walk over to our table.

"Guys this is Raphael, Raph this is Brooklyn, Leo, Nathan and that wobbling drunk is Cameron. This is Taylor, you've already met her. Well actually you didn't, because we were rather busy." She giggles.

I stand up and hold my hand out.

"Nice to meet you." I say.

"I'm going to take Cameron back to the hotel," Nathan says.

"Yeah, I'll give you a hand, Brooklyn you staying with the girls, we can handle this drunken ass if you want to stay?" Leo asks Brooklyn.

"Yeah I'm going to stay. Catch you later?" Brooklyn replies.

Once we say goodbye to the lads, Stacee sits back in her seat and Raphael joins us. We fall into an easy flow of conversations for the next two hours, then Brooklyn suggests we go to the nightclub, so we all agree.

The nightclub is packed and the music is blasting as we walk in. Stacee whispers something into Raph's ear, then pulls me in the direction of the ladies toilets, the music fades as we go enter. Stacee proceeds to enter one of the cubicles.

"Raph has asked me to go back to his room for a few drinks later, so I won't be staying in our room tonight. If you want to take Brooklyn back and have your own fun, you can." Stacee shouts through the toilet door.

"Okay thanks, but doubt that will happen, just be safe" I tell her as the cubicle door opens and she goes to the sink to wash her hands.

"Yeah I will be, now let's go find our men." She says, then opens the we door.

We find the lads by the bar, each holding a bottle of Smirnoff and a bottle of bud. Stacee starts swaying to the music that's currently blasting through the speakers.

"Come on, let's go and dance" She suggests.

So, we all down most of our drinks, before placing them on the bar and move towards the centre of the dancefloor where everyone is. Dirty by Christina Aguilera comes on, and I move my body to the beat of the music. Brooklyn dances behind me, with one arm wrapped around my waist, holding me against him as we move in sync. Trying to be sultry and sexy, I lift my left arm up and hook my hand around his neck. He leans down and kisses my neck, before he whispers in my ear.

"Do you want to get out of here?"

I nod and go to leave the dancefloor but he spins me around to face him. Before I can utter a word, I'm taken by surprise when he pulls me tight against him, I can feel how aroused he is. His lips are on mine in a flash, his hunger for more is shown in his body language.

Tenerife Temptation

Chapters Six

Justin Timberlake's Sexyback is blasting through the speakers and the disco lights flash in sync, the scene on the dancefloor is like one out of dirty dancing, the one with the water melons. The heat in the room is scorching from the lights and everyone's body heat. My body has a mind of its own, his hands are all over me as we dance. He spins me around and I lean in to his body. His mouth is feathering kisses all over my neck, he gently squeezes arse before he starts rubbing my leg.

Suddenly, I'm forced back to reality, my eyes spring open and I find a pair of the most gorgeous aqua blue eyes gazing back at me.

"Hi." I whisper, he smiles.

"Morning gorgeous," he says, then lifts his arm and gently runs his fingers along my cheek, before cupping my face.

I wasn't really dreaming all of that was I?

"Was I really in a nightclub, dancing like a porn star? "I ask, and he laughs.

"Yeah babe, it really happened."

Brooklyn confirms my dream was true. I quickly sit up and check for my clothes, I am still wearing what I had on last night. Turning to him, I take in his appearance, he's just wearing a pair of jeans with the top button open. As he sits up, he notices the frown on my face and panic in my eyes.

"We didn't do anything last night, in case that's what you were thinking."

I breathe a sigh of relief and flop backwards.

"Jesus, I thought..."

"I know what you were thinking Taylor but I can promise you that the only thing we did last night was dance and kiss before we came back here. Stacee disappeared with Raph. Then we continued making out before falling asleep and here we are," he explains then lays down beside me on his side. "You are so beautiful Taylor; can I kiss you?"

"Yes"

I say as he leans forward cupping the side of my face, his lips touch mine so tenderly. My eyes flutter close, my body is on fire. My heart feels like it's racing. After a few moments we slowly pull apart, both breathing heavily and I open my eyes. His hand still cups my face.

"Will you have dinner with me tonight, somewhere off the hotel site, just us?" he asks.

"I'd love to." I tell him and he leans in, placing a sweet kiss on my nose.

We are interrupted by a knock on the door, we pull apart and I swing my legs over the side of the bed, before getting up to answer it. I open the door to see Stacee holding her shoes in her one hand and bag in the other.

"Looks like you had fun, how is your head.?" I ask.

"My head is fine, it's the throbbing ache between my legs that hurts, his cock, it's massive…"

She pauses when she sees Brooklyn laying on my bed with his hands behind his back. His six pack abs glistening, on full display, my mouth waters at the sight of his toned body

"Well hello sexy, did you have as much fun as I did last night?" She asks Brooklyn.

He laughs, then he sits up, climbs off the bed, grabbing his shirt and walks over towards Stacee, while doing his button up on his jean's.

"Sorry babe, I never kiss and tell," he says, then winks at her, before walking up to me. He cups my face and devours my mouth like a man possessed. He then pulls away, leaving me gasping for air. Then he slips on his shoes and walks backwards to the door.

"I'll see you later, meet me by the bar at six. I'm going to find the lads and hang out for a bit," he explains before leaving the room.

"Holly shit T, that was freaking hot, that guy is carrying a major boner for you. Didn't he screw your brains out last night…?"

"Stacee, I am not going to dignify that with an answer. I'm going to jump in the shower before we go down for breakfast." I explain, then walk into the en suite and close the door behind me.

Love

After

breakfast, we decide we would go explore the beautiful island and take in the sights. We spend about an hour on the beach, before Stacee decides she wants to go to Venture to do some shopping.

We stroll through the shops picking up some souvenirs, I buy a few fridge magnets and some keyrings. While Stacee keeps picking things up and placing them back down, not sure if she wants to buy them or not.

"Oh, wow T, look at these" Stacee says, holding a bracelet with star and shells attached.

"That is cute, are you going to buy it?"

"Yeah I think I will," she replies before going in to buy it. When she comes back out, we continue walking, both of us notice an old man selling pictures of people he has drawn.

"We should do this; it would be an awesome way to remember this holiday." I say to Stacee.

We both agree to have our pictures drawn, I went first then Stacee. The pictures look amazing and we thank the man and pay him. We roll our pictures up and continue looking in the shops as we walk.

"What a beautiful view." A voice behind me says.

I look up from the postcards I am looking through and see Cameron and Brooklyn.

"How is your head Cameron? You were wasted last night." I say.

He laughs, "Yeah, heads fine. Had a big breakfast, so I'm ready to get back on the sesh." He replies cockily.

"You're crazy," Stacee tells him.

"Yeah well, the best cure for a hangover is to get back on it…"

Stacee cuts him off.

"You will end up spending the rest of the holiday in hospital with alcohol poisoning if you don't take a break and jump straight back on to drink. Especially after the state of you last night…"

"Whatever, you ain't my mother so you can save the lecture."

Brooklyn moves to stand in front of Cameron.

"Cam, you need to chill, Stacee is only saying what she thinks. There is no need to speak to her like that," he says defending Stacee.

Cameron shoves Brooklyn and storms off.

"Cameron, come on, don't be like that" Brooklyn shouts after him but he flips him the bird and ignores him.

"Sorry about him, he's been in a funny mood since last night, Stacee don't take any notice of him. He's just being a jackass; he will be gone for a few hours before he comes back."

"Is he okay? He seemed fine yesterday." Stacee asks.

"Yeah as far as I know but I'll speak to him about it later."

"Okay, well, have fun with that. T, I'm going to grab a juice over there" She says before saying bye to Brooklyn, then leaves us alone.

"Are you still coming to dinner with me later?" He asks, stepping closer to me before catching my hands in his.

"Yeah, I'll have dinner with you, I'm looking forward to it."

He lifts my hand up to his lips and kisses it.

"Me too, I can't wait to have you all to myself. I'll be in the bar at six, waiting." He adds before he drops my hands and walks off in the direction Cameron went.

Stacee appears out of nowhere as I'm watching Brooklyn's back disappear.

"Well, he's just like one of the characters out of those books you love to read. A real-life prince charming, who new Tenerife would have temptations for us both," she giggles.

Chapter Seven

"Stacee are you sure you don't mind me ditching you to go out with Brooklyn?" I ask as I stare at my reflection in the en suite mirror as I apply some lip gloss, while only dressed in my bra and panties. My hair is up in a clip, so it's out of the way.

"T, I'm positive I'll be fine, plus it's not as if I will be on my own, Raph is coming up, so I'll have my hands busy," she replies with a smirk on her face.

"Oh my God Stacee, I don't want to know anymore. I'm so nervous but I don't know why, it's not as if it's the first time we would be alone…"

"T, you're overthinking things, it is just a dinner date. You need to chill out, seriously Brooklyn seems like a nice guy. God, he didn't even try to take advantage of you the other night…"

"How do you know?" I question.

"Taylor you are my best friend, of course I know you didn't fuck his brains out, otherwise you would be chirpy as a sparrow on a winter's morning. Last time you slept with a guy was a year ago, Thomas, if I remember right. You were walking around like you won the lottery. Always smiling and chirpy." She teases.

"Okay, fine your right…."

"I know, I'm usually always right about these things."

"Well, I better shift my arse and finish getting ready." I say while grabbing my black, floral dress off the door, before taking it off the hanger and gently lifting it over my head.

Trying not to disturb my hair, I poke my arms through the thin black straps, as the dress falls down my body.

"What do you think Stacee, do I look okay?" I ask turning to face her.

"T, you look stunning, you'll knock him dead, Now go get your man." She says as she passes me my bag from the corner of the sink and pushes me towards the hotel room door.

"Thanks, Stacee, see you later." I say as I leave the room.

My heart feels like it's coming out of my chest, my hands are sweaty and trembling. I'm not normally nervous when I go on dates but for some reason, I am this time as I walk down from my room to the bar in the lobby. As I enter the lobby, I look across to the bar opposite for Brooklyn, he is stood by there with his back to me. He must of sense someone watching him because he turns around, his eyes meet mine and he smiles as he walks towards me.

"You look beautiful Taylor; do you want a drink first or should we go straight for food?"

"Would you mind if we go for food rather than stay here.?"

"Not at all babe. Let's go"

He says as he takes my hand and lifts it up to his lips before kissing it. Brooklyn leads me out of the hotel, we walk about for ten minutes before we stop outside a restaurant called Manuel's. Brooklyn pulls the door open and holds is open for me.

"Thanks." I say as I walk in to the restaurant.

The maître d greets us before taking us over to a table set for two. Brooklyn pulls the chair out for me to sit on before he takes a seat himself. A waiter comes over and takes our drinks order, we both decide to have a glass of white wine. The waiter walks off to get our drinks, leaving us to have a look at the menu.

"Wow this place is beautiful, this menu looks amazing but I don't know what to have. Do you know what you are having?"

"I know, there is so much to choose from. Do I have traditional Spanish food or go with something we would eat back home?" he laughs.

"I know what you mean, I feel like I should try some traditional Spanish food, get out of my comfort zone. I'm leaning towards Spanish sausage and chips or Paella."

"The Paella does sound nice though. Mmm, I think I will have that and order side of chips, do you want to share a portion of chips?" he asks, so I nod.

"Yeah that sound good." I reply just as the waiter brings our drinks over.

"Are you ready to order?" he asks.

Brooklyn glances across to me and I nod in approval.

"Yes, we are. Taylor, what would you like to eat?"

"I'll have the Paella Valenciana, is that the one with just the meats in?" I ask the waiter.

"Yes madam, that is correct. The Paella de Marsico's is the seafood one and Paella Mixta is the dish with a combination of both." he explains.

"Oh, that's great, thank you."

"I will have the same as my lady and can we have a side order of chips to share please." Brooklyn adds as the waiter writes our orders down on a notepad.

"Will that be all Sir, Madam?"

"Yes, thank you." We say in unison.

The waiter walks away with our order leaving us alone, I lift my wine glass up and take a sip before placing it back down. Brooklyn does the same, then places his glass on the table before reaching across the table and catches both my hands in his.

"So, Taylor tell me about yourself?" he asks as his thumbs rub the back of my hands.

"Well, I finished my final year in college, training to be a teaching assistant. Actually both myself and Stacee have just finished, this holiday is a celebration for all the hard work we put in."

"So, do you know what you are going to do now you have finished the course?" he asks.

"Well, I found out that I have a job interview in a local high school when we go back, so I'm really hoping I will get it…"

"I'm sure you will, you seem to have a good head on your shoulders."

"Can you tell me about yourself?"

"Oh, not much to tell really, I work in a hotel, my parents are retired and live down in Devon. I have a younger sister Bethany and a brother Jacob, he's a few years older than me," he replies just as the waiter brings our food over.

He let's go of my hands as the food is placed on the table."

"Thank you." we both say.

"Enjoy your food." The waiter says then leaves.

"This smells lovely." I say.

"Yes, it does look delicious," he replies before we both start eating. As we each the conversation continues, both choosing easy topics to discuss.

After we are done, the waiter comes back and clears the dishes away, once the waiter leaves, Brooklyn catches my hands again.

"So, Taylor do you have any brothers or sisters?"

"Yes, I have one brother, Daniel, he's thirty-six and a manager for one of the biggest hotels in Cardiff. Mum died when I was small but dad still lives in Cardiff, he loves to play golf."

"Is that where you are from Cardiff?"

"Yeah, I'm a Cardiff girl through and though. What about you where are you from?"

"I'm originally from London but I'm currently all over the place looking at houses. I was living with Jacob for a while but he's decided he wants to travel, so he's given a month's notice on his flat in Manchester. I had no choice but to move back home with my parents, that is until I find something more permanent."

"Wow that sucks, couldn't you have taken over his lease while your brother went off travelling?"

He shakes his head, "Nah once Jacob sets his mind on something, he is too damn stubborn and won't change it. Do you want to go for a walk?"

"Sure, I'd like that, thank you for dinner Brooklyn. I've enjoyed this meal."

He waves at the waiter for the bill.

"The night isn't over yet Taylor, it's only just starting." he replies with a wink.

The waiter hands him the bill, Brooklyn takes out his wallet and places some cash on the table, then he stands.

"Ready?" he asks while holding out his hand out, I nod, stand up and place my hand in his.

We leave the restaurant holding hands and walk into the Venture complex.

"This place is amazing; I still haven't had a proper look around this place, when me and Stacee were here earlier. We did a bit of shopping before we saw you and Cameron. Then we had our pictures drawn by the old guy over there as a way to remember this place."

"You still have a few days left before you go home, plenty of time to see it all."

"Yeah, I guess so, we are going on that water park excursion tomorrow, so we probably won't get back to the hotel until around dinner time.

"Aww that a shame I was hoping I could kidnap you again tomorrow." he says pretending to pout.

I laugh, "You'll be busy with the lads, you'll probably won't notice I'm not there. I forgot to ask you; did you find Cameron before?"

"Yeah, he was in a pissy mood all day. When we were in the room, he said he had the hots for your friend but she was giving him mixed signals and she hooked up with that other guy."

"You mean Raphael?"

He nods.

"Yeah, she's become very cosy with him."

"Let's forget our friends drama, come on I have an idea," he says as he pulls me towards the old guy, who did the drawings of me and Stacee earlier.

"Let's have one together? I want one to remember you by."

I agree and we sit there for the next thirty minutes while the old man draws our picture. Once he's done, Brooklyn takes some money out and pays the guy, he then whispers something and the old man nods.

"What did you ask him?" I ask, but he just smirks and takes out his phone, before passing it to the old man who is now standing.

"Come here Taylor," Brooklyn says as he stands behind me, wrapping his arms around my waist. "This lovely man is going to take our photo with my phone."

We both smile for the photo. He then turns me to face him and kisses me, before he walking over to the man to thank him, and give him some more money. The old man packs his stuff away and walks away.

"Now I can see your face all the time, do you have your phone with you?

"Yes," I tell him, take it out of my bag and unlock it before handing it to over. He types a few times on his phone, then does the same on mine before he hands it back to me.

"I've just sent you the photos the old guy just took and added my number to your phone. As well as saving yours to mine." He says then hands my phone back.

"You really are full of surprises Brooklyn; it's going to be hard saying goodbye when the holiday ends." I say with a sad tone.

"Taylor, the night is young. Let's forget about the goodbyes and focus on what's happening now."

"You really are a real-life prince charming, like out of the books I read."

"Babe, you have no idea."

Tenerife Temptation

Chapter Eight

"Wake up sleeping beauty, we need to go down for breakfast. The bus taking us to the Aqua park will be here soon." Stacee calls.

I spring up out of bed.

"Balls. What time is it?" I ask as I swing my legs over the edge of the bed.

"It's only eight," Stacee replies.

"Are you serious." I groan and flop backwards on the bed.

"So how was your dinner date with Mr Dreamy?" Stacee asks as she jumps on the bed beside me.

"Why are you so hyper this morning, it's still early?" I moan.

"I'm not hyper, I am just excited to go to the Aqua park later and I want to know how your date went."

I sit up and face her.

"You are so annoying. Fine, I'll tell you. Brooklyn was sweet and nothing but the perfect gentleman last night. We talked, he's told me he has a younger sister and an older brother. He asked me about my family and oh, where's my phone?" I ask and she grabs it from the table where it was on charge.

"Thanks, remember when we has our pictures drawn by that old guy?"

She nods.

"Well Brooklyn wanted us to have one done so he could remember me by. Once the old man had finished, Brooklyn asked him to take a photo of us using his phone. He sent me a few pictures as well, so I'd have copies." I explain as I unlock my phone and scroll through until I find the photos. I turn the phone and show her.

"Aww, you look so cute together, you're like the perfect couple. He has that look in his eyes, where he's falling for you big time. So, when are you going to see him again?"

"I think you're wrong; how can you fall for someone in a space of a few days?"

"T, it doesn't matter if it's a few days or a few months, when you fall in love you know. Looking at that photo of the both of you, I'd say he's definitely on his way for falling head over heels for you. So, are you seeing him again?"

"Not sure, I said we were off to the water park today, so I said I'd let him know when we got back. I'm going to have a quick shower before we go down to breakfast." I tell her, then plug my phone back on charge before jumping in the shower.

Love

Two hours later, we arrive at the Aqua park, it didn't take us long to get there, it was situated up on the mountains. We climb off the bus and go through the check in desk. The woman on the desk places yellow wrist bands on our wrists to show we have paid and if we need to step outside the water park. Once everyone is checked in, we are allowed to enter the water park; our bus was the first one to arrive, so the park was empty. We manage to locate the lockers which are beside the toilets and store our bags, making sure that we have our towels and sun cream with us. We place them on a sun lounger before going on the biggest water ride in the park. Grabbing a rubber ring, we climb the steps and place the rubber rings in place.

"Ready?" I say to Stacee.

"Let's go." She yells and we both push off, speeding down the slides on the rubber rings.

We launch into the air and drop into the water with a massive splash. The ring goes one way and I go the other. I kick my feet and push up from the water, gasping for air and trying to catch my breath. I swim over to grab the rubber ring and climb out just as Stacee appears and swims to get hers, before joining me.

"That was freaking awesome, I want to do that again." she shouts.

We go on it two more times before we move on to another ride. Stacee goes first down the slide and ten minutes after, the guy who watches the ride for safety reasons, lets me go. As I fly down this tube, it bends before a massive drop comes out of nowhere and I'm suddenly thrown into the pool. It takes me a few minutes for me to get my bearings, I swim out of the pool and climb out. I notice that Stacee is talking to two lads, I can't take her anywhere, she's like a boy magnet. I walk over to them.

"Hey T, look who I bumped into, its Jake from the plane and his friend Adam," she grins.

"Oh yeah, hey guys. How is your holiday going?" I ask.

"It's been good but I'm glad I bumped into you girls again, how has your holiday been?" Jake asks.

"Yeah we are having a good time."

"You girls fancy hanging out, while we are all here?" Adam asks.

We all agree before heading off around the park in search of more rides.

Stacee goes on a slide with Adam, so I decide to go grab mine and Stacee's purses so we could go get something to eat.

"So, Taylor, do you and Stacee fancy meeting up tonight?" Jake asks.

"Yeah maybe, are you staying far from Venture?"

"Actually, no our hotel is opposite, what about you, are you far from there?"

"Our hotel is right behind it, we have been down a few times, not been on the upper level yet though."

"Well, do you want to come to Fire with us later? It's a bar and nightclub in one. It's on the upper level of Venture." He explains.

"Oh okay, I didn't know there was more than one nightclub, we went to one a couple of nights ago it was packed in there."

"I know the one you are talking about, I've been in there twice, not a fan of that place, my younger brother hangs out there. We came here together but his friends booked a different hotel to mine and my friends. He's a prick to be honest, I wish we went to a different resort."

"Oh, that bad huh" I say just as Stacee and Adam come back.

"Hey kids what are you talking about?" Stacee asks.

"I just asked Taylor if you girls fancied joining us tonight at Fire, it's a bar and nightclub on the upper level of Venture." Jake explains.

"Ooh sounds fun, we will come for sure. What time and where should we meet you both?" She asks him, I glare at her.

"Do you know where the old man who does the drawings sits?" he asks

"Yeah, we know."

"Meet us by there at seven-thirty."

"Sounds like a plan, let's go get some food T." Stacee says grabbing my arm before pulling me towards the food hut.

"What was that just now? You know Brooklyn wanted to catch up later." I explain as I shake my arm from her grasp.

We stop in front of the food hut and look at the menu.

"Look T, Brooklyn is dreamy I won't deny it but you met Jake on the plane. He was really nice and I think we should go hang out with them tonight. Send Brooklyn a text and just say we have plans, so you'll meet up with him tomorrow instead," she says before ordering herself a milkshake and a hamburger.

I give in and order the same as Stacee before pulling out my phone and sending Brooklyn a text like she suggests. We walk back over to where the lads are sitting and eat our food and drinks. We spend the rest of the afternoon with Jake and Adam.

Before we know it, it's time to make our way back to the bus. Just before we go on our own buses, Jake asks one of the passengers, a man if he would take our photo with his phone, so we all get together and have our photo taken.

"Thanks man." Jake says to the guy as he hands phone back.

"Hey Taylor, do you have your phone with you?"

"Yeah I do." I say, pulling my phone out of my bag.

I unlock it before handing it to him, he presses a few buttons on his phone and then on mine, before handing it back to me.

"There, now you have the photo and I have your phone number," he winks.

"Guess we will see you later then." Stacee adds, before she pulls me over to the bus.

Tenerife Temptation

I wave to Jake and Adam before climbing on.

Chapter Nine

"Did you send Brooklyn a text before?" Stacee asks from beside me on the bus.

"Yeah, I have and I'm still pissed off with you by the way. Jake's nice but I don't want to go leading him on, when I really like Brooklyn. It's not fair or right…"

"Oh, get over it T, we're just going for a few drinks and have a good time in the process, what's wrong with that huh? Nothing that's what so put on your big girl panties and suck it up." She tells me, then pulls out her earphones and phone from her bag and plugs them in and placing them in her ears, ending our conversation.

I pull out my phone from my bag and scroll through until I came to my photo gallery and click on it. The photo of myself, Stacee, Adam and Jake fills the screen. From a distance it looks like we are a group of friends, so why am I having such a hard time agreeing to go for drinks with them. I scroll past it until I come to the photos of myself and Brooklyn. At first glance it looks like we are a proper couple. The way his arms wrap around my waist, holding me kind of possessively. The way I lean into his touch, maybe if we had longer together, we could get to know each other better. My phone vibrates, it's a text from Jake.

Had fun today hanging out with you and Stacee, looking forward to drinks later x.

I smile, maybe it won't be a bad idea after all. I send him a quick text back.

Me to, see you later.

I hit send then put my phone away.

We have just left the hotel as we walk to Venture, Stacee pauses at the top of the steps

"T, are you going to chill out tonight and have a good time or are you going to be a moody bitch?"

I raise my eyebrows at her tone.

"Stacee, I said I will have fun okay but do me a favour and don't try and push me and Jake together."

"Okay fine, that's good enough for me. Let's go before they think we've stood them up," she says as she walks off ahead.

Just as we approach the old man who does the drawings, I notice Jake and Adam walking from the other side of the complex. Adam is wearing a white T shirt and black trousers, while Jake wears a white, short sleeved shirt and navy trousers.

"Stacee do I look okay?" I ask glanced down at myself.

I decided to wear a white skirt with a black thin lace evening top and Stacee his wearing her white, hot pants and matching white vest top.

"T, you look stunning as always, now come on, I can see the guys." She says as the lads spot us.

Stacee waves and they both wave back, I smile at as we walk towards each other.

"You girls look beautiful, are you ready to get your dance shoes on?" Adam asks as he takes in Stacee's outfit.

He looks like a horny teenager when he sees a girl he fancies.

"I could use a few drinks before I hit the dance floor." I say as I walk past Stacee to where Jake is standing.

"You and me both baby..." Jake agrees before he leads the way to Fire.

Stacee sticks with Adam while we walk, I glance back at her a few times and she's openly flirting with Adam. Fire is already busy when we walk in.

"Taylor, what do you want to drink?" Jake asks.

I take in my surroundings and answer Jake.

"I'll have a WKD blue please."

"Stacee what do you want?" he asks.

"Vodka and coke please." she replies, just as Adam whispers something in her ear, then walks off with Jake to the bar.

"Stacee what is going on with you and Adam? You only met him a few hours ago and you are already flirting with the guy." I say as she rolls her eyes.

"Oh my god T, you are not my mother, you're supposed to be my friend. So, will you stop acting like you are my mother and just be my friend," she replies with a scowl, just as the lads come back with our drinks.

"Here you go ladies" Jake says holding out our drinks.

"Thanks." We say in unison.

Stacee downs here drink in one.

"Hey Adam, fancy a dance?" she asks and winks at him.

"Hell yes," he says before gulping down over half of his bottle before handing it to Jake. "Let's go baby," he says holding his hand toward her, she eagerly takes it and they go off into the crowd.

Jake places Adam's drink on the nearest table and comes closer to me.

"Taylor, I have a confession."

"Oh, and what's that."

He moves closer to my ear and the hairs on the back of my neck prick up.

"I've wanted to get you alone ever since I first saw you on the plane, I've wanted to kiss you."

My whole body is instantly covered in goose bumps. He pulls back and gazes into my eyes. Taking my drink out of my hand, he pulls me towards the dance floor, just as a Dirty by Christina arugula comes on. Jake pulls me towards him and we both start dancing. The song changes and I turn to Jake.

"I need to get a drink and some air, it's really hot in here."

We both walk to the bar to grab a drink, before going out onto the balcony that overlooks the bottom level.

"So, Jake tell me about your brother, you mentioned before you came here with him but you aren't in the same hotels."

He takes a few gulps of his bottle of bud before he turns to look at me.

"Well, we originally planned this holiday a while ago but I recently found out something he does that nobody else knows. Even our parents think he's a goody two shoes. If they only knew the truth… Ah fuck, I don't want to waste time talking about him while I have a beautiful girl in my presence," he replies before taking another mouthful from his bottle.

"So, tell me about yourself."

We spend the next hour talking, I tell him about my family and my job. He tells me he's travelling around a lot; he mentions he's got a younger sister who he's really close to.

"There you are, why are you out here, the bar is in there." Stacee slurs, grabs my hand, and pulls me back inside. She is totally rat-arsed.

Love

Two

hours later, she is wobbling all over the place.

I don't know what she's been drinking, but she's a total mess. I decided a hour ago to switch my drink from WKD blue to coke. After a few glasses, I've gone from slightly tipsy to sober.

"I think I'd better take Stacee back to the hotel."

"Do you want us to walk you back?" Jake asks.

I shake my head.

"No thanks, I'll be okay. I'm used to carrying her home after a night on the town."

"Okay, if you are sure I'll take Adam to the bar, otherwise he will want to follow you back; I think he has the hots for her."

Jake goes up to the dancefloor and whispers into Adam's ear, then they walk to the bar. I take that as my chance to grab Stacee, lead her off the dancefloor and tell her a little white lie. I explain that Raph is waiting for her. That puts a rocket in her step as we walk out of the club and towards the steps to the hotel. We are nearly at the top of the steps when I notice Raphael standing, talking on his phone. When he sees us, he hangs up.

"Stacee my darling, how was your night?" He asks her but she just mumbles and closes her eyes.

"Miss Taylor, can I help?" he asks me as he catches her other side.

"Yes, please Raph, she's a little drunk." I explain.

He helps me all the way up to the hotel room. As I unlock the door, he lifts Stacee up into his arms and carries her in the room, before placing her gently on the bed. He then takes off her wedges, before lifting her slightly and pulling the blanket over her. He then walks over to the door and I follow him.

"Thank you for your help tonight."

"It wasn't any trouble, when she wakes up tell her to text me, so I know she's okay."

I agree to tell her, before saying goodnight and closing the door behind him.

Chapter Ten

The sound of something crashing on the floor close by wakes me up. It feels like I haven't long fallen asleep, after Raph left last night, Stacee started snoring like she usually does. She's always does when she's been drinking Vodka all night, so I sat on the balcony for a good hour last night playing a game on my phone.

Lifting my head, I glance across to Stacee's bed, she's out cold, sleeping on her stomach. Throwing back the blanket, I swing both feet over the edge of the bed. I reach over and check my phone while it's on charge, it's just gone seven in the morning. I yawn and stretch, before standing up and walking out onto the balcony and glance down at the pool area in front of me. There is nobody in or near it.

"Hey did I wake you?"

A voice says from the other side of the partitioning wall on the balcony.

"Jesus." I say, jumping a mile.

A girl with jet black hair leans over the wall.

"Hey sorry for scaring you. I'm so clumsy, I just dropped my makeup bag as I was trying to carry to many things all at once. Oh, I'm Brie but the way"

I walk over to her and hold my hand out.

"I'm Taylor, I think I met your sister the other morning, Suzy."

At the sound of her name she appears the other side of Brie.

"Hey Taylor, Brie I swear you could wake the dead with the noise you make." she tells her sister.

"Oh, shut up it wasn't that loud. So Taylor what are you doing today?" Brie asks.

"I'm not sure, my friend was absolutely paralytic last night, I had to carry her back from Fire and put her to bed."

"Well in that case, you should come with us to the beach, we are going straight after breakfast. You should leave your friend a note to tell her where you are going and come with us." Brie suggests.

"You know what, sod it, I'm in. I'll go get changed, grab my bag, then I'll knock for you when I'm done."

"Awesome, oh and Taylor, make sure you grab some extra bottles of water at breakfast to take with you to the beach." Brie adds before they both disappear.

I step back into the hotel room and scribble a quick note on a piece of paper from my bag and place it on the table by Stacee's bed. I change into my black bikini and put my red shorts and white t shirt on top, then run the brush through my hair, before sticking it up in a messy bun. I grab my towel and sun creams and shove them inside my big beach bag, along with my purse, phone, and my room key. Slipping my feet into my flip flops, I open the door and go knock on next door for Brie and Suzy.

Love

Forty minutes later, we were done with breakfast and we are walking towards the beach.

"So, have you been to the beach a lot since you arrived here?" I ask them both.

Brie glances at me

"Yeah, we have been a few times, plus, the view is amazing and I don't mean the sea either" Brie says wiggling her eyebrows.

"Oh, okay."

"Just ignore my sister, she's a perv, there is a group of lads that always come to the beach and Brie loves to flirt with them. She has her eye on this one lad but he hasn't batted an eyelid, despite her many attempts to get his attention." Suzy says giggling.

I glance at Brie and she breaks into a smile.

"What can I say, I need to up my game and do more, so come on let hustle our asses to the beach. We are not far, it's just down the road."

As we reach an road between a hotel and some tourist shops, the beach comes in to view, so we make out way down. Just before we walk on to the sand, Brie and Suzy take their flip flops off, before stepping on, I do the same and follow them.

"Follow me this way, I know the perfect spot." Brie orders.

She walks for about ten minutes before stopping, taking her towel out of her bag, laying it out on the sand and sitting on it. Both myself and Suzy do the same and place ours either side of Brie. I place my flip flops at the bottom of my towel and dig in my bag for my sun cream and squirt some into my hand then start rubbing it into my arms. Brie wastes no time in stripping out of her shorts and vest top, down to her red bikini. Suzy isn't like her sister, she's not as eager to reveal her body. She just takes off her top and sits there in a pair of black shorts and navy swimsuit.

"So, Taylor, have you met any Spanish hunks since you have been here?" Brie asks.

I smile and think about Brooklyn and Jake.

"Not Spanish but I have met a couple of hunks." I reply before taking my vest top off and laying down on my stomach.

"Ooo, tell us more?" Suzy adds.

"Well on my flight over, this guy sat in the same row as me and Stacee, then we bump into him again at the Aqua park yesterday. He was with his friend and asked me and Stacee out for drinks. So Stacee jumped at his invitation and wanted to set me up, but I wasn't so sure myself. A few days after we arrived here, this guy came up to me while I was sat in the hotel lobby reading and well, we kinda of hit it off. I've seen him a few times."

"Oh wow, so you have two potential Tenerife Temptations." Brie says and I laugh.

"I guess so, what about you two, have you met any guys, apart the guy you mentioned earlier.?"

"I'm not looking to hook up with anyone. When I find someone, I'm into, I want there to be spark or a zing if you like. I'm just here to have a good time and gain a tan, also, if a guy does come on to me, I'm not going ignore him." Suzy replies.

"Oh my God Suzy, you read way to many romance books, real life ain't like it is in a book. Let me tell you now, if you want a guy, you just got to go get him. Draw his attention in something super sexy and let out your inner siren. My sister is a romantic book nerd, she thinks all men should be like they are in the books she reads. I however, don't. I want a man who will rock my world, show me his wild and sexy side. I want a man to seduce and charm the knickers off me…"

Suzy cuts her off.

"In other words, she wants a hunk who will screw her brains out until she can't walk."

Brie turns around and lays down on her stomach.

"Well duh, all girls want that," she says before she closes her eyes.

The beach is quiet at the moment, there are a few people here sunbathing.

We spend the next hour and half soaking up the sun and talking. My eyes are closed when a group of male voices catches my attention. So, I turn over and sit up to have a look, there are three guys laughing as they lay on their towels, all have sunglasses on. They sound familiar but I don't know where from. Feeling the heat, I take off my shorts revealing my full bikini.

"Hey, girls, do either of you want an ice cream?"

I want something to cool me down, so I'm going to grab one."

Suzy stands up, taking off her shorts before digging through her bag and pulling out her purse.

"Yeah, I'll come I fancy one too, Brie you want anything?"

"No thanks, I'm going to go for a dip in the sea in a bit," she says.

So we leave her there and we walk up to the little hut by the entrance to the beachfront.

"You will have to ignore my sister, she's man crazy at the moment, she's on the rebound. She split with her boyfriend a month before we came here as she caught him sleeping with his supervisor one night. It was a total dick thing to do and well ever since then, she's been going out trying to hook up with different guys." Suzy explains.

"Ah okay, makes sense. Brie mentioned you like to read as well; do you have any particular author you like to read?" I ask her while we order and pay for our ice creams.

"I have a few, I love Rachel Van Dyken's, Seaside series and I am obsessed with Kendall Greys, Strings book. Oh my god now if Shades, the male character was real oh, holy hell, the things I'd do with that guy."

"Is the book that good then?"

"Oh yes definitely, if you haven't read it, then you seriously need to. I've also found this new author called BJ. Weston. He writes mostly vampire and werewolf books, but he's just published two new ones. One book is set on an island, where two people are stranded. I'm half way through it now. You should look up the author up and see if you like the sound of his books," she suggests as we make our way back to our towels.

Chapter Eleven

When we get back, Brie was over by the lads that I had heard earlier. The way she was moving her body it looks like she's trying to seduce him. Suzy and I sit on our towels watching the show of Brie trying to flirt with one of the guys, while we eat our ice creams.

"She's determined to get her claws into that guy but he's not paying her any attention." Suzy says as she finishes her cone.

The one guy gets up, takes off his sunglasses and tosses them on to his towel. He picks Brie up, throwing her over his shoulders and carries her to the sea, before dunking her and himself underwater. She laughs before swimming back to shore and walks back to where we are sitting.

"He's crazy, if I didn't fancy his friend so bad, I would see how far I could take things with him while we are on holiday." Brie says as she grabs a smaller towel from her bag and begins drying herself, before sitting back down.

"Which one of the guys do you have a thing for?" I ask her.

"There he is just coming out of the sea in a pair of black swimming shorts," she replies pointing at the sea.

I glance up to where she's pointing, my jaw falls open as my heart starts to flutter and my eyes go wide. Its Brooklyn.

"Holy cow."

"I know right, he is so hot." Brie says as he notices me and smiles before he walks towards us.

"Oh my God, he's coming over." Brie squeals.

He holds his hand out towards me and I take it, Brie and Suzy stare from beside me as I take it.

"Hey beautiful." He says before he leans in and kisses me in front of everyone, then we break apart.

"Hey Brooklyn, have you met Brie and Suzy?" I ask motioning towards the girls.

I take a quick look at Brie's reaction; she looks like a goldfish with her mouth open.

"Oh, hey girls nice to meet you both."

"Hey Brooklyn, nice to meet you as well. So, are you Taylor's boyfriend?" Suzy asks him as she and Brie stand up.

"No, I met Taylor in the lobby of our hotel after I been watching her earlier on in the day, when she had her head in the Abbi Glines book she was glued to. I know that makes me sound like a stalker but I couldn't hold back any longer, I really wanted to meet the girl who spent over two hours sitting poolside with her head in a book."

"Aww that's sweet…" Suzy was saying until Brie cuts her off.

"I'm going for a walk." Brie says and walks off.

"Ignore Brie, she's in a mood, when she calms down, she will come back." Suzy explains

"Do you want to come for a swim with me girls?" Brooklyn asks me and Suzy.

"Thanks, but I'll pass, I only swim in pools, you never know what's in the sea, but you two can go ahead. I'm going to read for a while." Suzy replies.

"I guess a swim sounds good," I tell him.

He catches my hand as we walk into the sea, we both drop our hands before leaning forward and start swimming.

After a while, I decide that I just want to lay on my back in the shallow part of the water, just before it meets the sand. I watch Brooklyn as he swims, then close my eyes and enjoy the heat on my face and my chest. The water splashes around me as people walk in the water.

"God you are breath-taking, the way you are laying in the shallow part of the sea as the water hits your body, it makes you look like a swimwear model, so sexy." A voice says.

I open my eyes to see Brooklyn staring at my body and I giggle.

"I don't look like a model; those girls have amazing figures," I reply as he leans down, picks me up out of the sea and carries me until we are on the sand. He stands me up but doesn't move his arms from around my body, holding me against his.

"I want to be alone with you, can you come with me for a little rock climb?"

"Yeah, I can, but what about my friends? I ask breathlessly.

"Tell them you will see them later and that I will walk you back to the hotel. Grab your things and I'll go grab mine, then we can go for a walk to a place I know."

"Yeah okay."

He drops his arms from around me and I walk back over to Suzy who is still reading.

"Hey Suzy, would you mind if I go off with Brooklyn for a walk? He wants to take me somewhere; I know I came here with you and Brie but..."

"Taylor, if I hand a hunk like that who was crazy about me, the way Brooklyn seems to be about you, I sure as hell wouldn't be sat on the beach. Go have fun and I'm sorry about my moody sister, she's just jealous that he's into you and not her," she says with a smile.

"Okay if you are sure, can you tell Brie I didn't mean for things to happen like they have. Maybe we can go for a drink in the hotel either tonight or tomorrow.?"

I suggest as I pull on my shorts and stuff my top in my bag, then pick up my towel, give it a little shake place it in my bag. Once I made sure I had everything, I place my bag on my shoulder, I pick up my flip flops and walk over to where Brooklyn is stood talking to his friends. I didn't notice before that it was Leo, Nathan, and Cameron. Those were the voices that sounded familiar earlier but I couldn't see them. Brooklyn turns as I approached.

"Are you ready Taylor?" He asks and I nod. "Okay, I'm me too," he says and catches my free hand and leads me off the beach.

He asks me about Stacee and how our night was last night. I explain that we went dancing at another club and how she tried to set me up with some guy that we met on the plane, after seeing him at the Aqua park. I also told him I had to carry her back to the hotel as she was totally pissed, but we met Raph on the way and he helped me with her.

We don't end up going too far from the beach, we reach a rocky path that leads to a secluded beach. It's covered with mostly rocks and a small section of white sand.

"Over here, I found this place yesterday, nobody comes down here, it's kind of like a private beach." He says as we stop by a big cluster of massive rocks, that look like giant creamy coloured pebbles.

He climbs up on to one, holds his hand out for me and I climb up, following him. He pulls the towel he had over his shoulder and places it on top of the rocks. I do the same taking my towel out of my bag and place it by his. Pulling his top from the back of his shorts, he folds it up like a pillow, then sits on top of his towel.

"What is this place?" I ask, glancing around.

Brooklyn catches my hand and pulls me to sit between his legs. My heart starts fluttering, I feel things I don't normally do, when it's just us and nobody else is around.

"I'm not sure, I don't think many people know about this place." he replies, he pauses for a second, then continues, "Taylor, I know we both fly home soon but I'd really like to see you again. My friends think I'm crazy and

I probably am, but the truth is you are a breath of fresh air. You are nothing like the girls I'm used to. I wanted to bring you here to just spend time with you alone. I'm falling for you Taylor; you don't have to say anything, I just wanted to tell you," he confesses.

I'm at a loss for words, that wasn't what I was expecting, and my breath hitches. Everyone else said they could see he was falling for me but I think I've been too oblivious to see it. I move from between his legs to sit on the towel beside him.

"Brooklyn, I don't know what to say." I reply, but he doesn't say a word, instead he brushes his fingers along my cheeks. I close my eyes at the tenderness.

"Brooklyn..."

Instead of words, I show him what I'm feeling, I lean over to him, cupping his face with both hands and kiss him. He moans into my mouth, then grabs my waist, pulling me on top of him, and his back hits the rocks. Pausing, I put my hands onto his chest to push myself to sit up and straddle him, while I gasp for breath and gaze into his eyes. His eyes are glistening with lust and fire. He wants me as much as I want him, maybe even more but there is something stopping him, he's holding back.

"Baby, I ...Fuck it," he says.

Both his hands reach out and cup my face, pulling me to him. His lips smash against mine as his tongue slips into my mouth and dances with my tongue. His one hand drops from my face, then slips it into the back of my shorts, inside under my bikini bottoms and squeezes my bum cheeks slightly. My body is on fire, I want more. His arousal is evident, as his dick pokes my stomach from inside his shorts. He doesn't make a move to free himself from his confines, instead he's like a hungry lion, devouring my mouth and getting dick is getting harder.

Chapter Twelve

We spent three hours on the rocks kissing and talking, before making our way back to the hotel. The sun begins to go down as we get back to the hotel. The smells of rich curries and other spices fill the air as we walk into the lobby, hand in hand.

"Come back to my room with me so I can change for dinner and then I'll come to your room with you." Brooklyn asks as we approach the lift.

"I think I'd better go straight to my room, Stacee is probably pissed off that I've left her alone all day." I explain as the lift opens.

We step into the lift and Brooklyn presses his floor number and I press mine.

"I've loved spending the day with you Brooklyn, you are one of the nicest guys I've met in a long time. I wish I didn't have to go home on Sunday morning." I tell him, just as my phone goes off.

Opening my bag, I reach in and pull out my phone, its Stacee.

"Hey Stacee, I'm on my way up to the room now, I'll explains when I get there." I tell her then hang up.

The lift reaches my floor and the doors open.

"Thank you for today." I tell him, then kiss him on the cheek and walk out towards my room.

Pulling out my key card, I place it in the lock, wait for it to turn green and I push the door open. Stacee is sitting on the bed, she looks pissed off, her are arms crossed and she has a scowl on her face.

"Look Stacee, I'm sorry I left you on your own all day, but that little stunt you pulled yesterday with trying to set me up with Jake, knowing full well I really liked Brooklyn, pissed me off. I didn't stand in the way when you threw yourself at the first guy you met and jumped straight into bed with him did I? No, I didn't, you really annoyed me, that's why I went off with Brie and Suzy, because I wanted to have some fun." I shout.

I was being a major bitch but I didn't care. I had enough, Stacee was meant to be my best friend but she's been acting like we are nothing. My chest hurts and my eyes start to burn like they do when I feel like I am about to cry. I dump my bag on my bed, plug my phone in to charge, then grab some clean clothes and jump in the shower. Normally I take ages but today I just wanted a quick shower.

Within twenty minutes I am done, I climb out and dry my body, then put on my red flowery dress and black sandals. Using the towel, I dry my hair as best I can, then run the brush through it. I throw it up in my clip while it's still slightly damp. I apply some lip gloss and squirt a little perfume from the bottle I had left in the en suite. Once I am done, I open the door of the en suite, walk over to my bed and empty the contents of my all over it. Picking up my purse, book, and body spray, I throw them back in, then I go back into the en suite to grab my brush and perfume, and add them to my bag. I storm past Stacee, who is still in a mood, grab my phone from the charger and room key, then walk out of the hotel room and go down to dinner on my own.

The dining area is a lot more busier compared to last time. I decide to try some Spanish chicken in red sauce and mushroom rice, then go find myself a seat. Finding a table hidden in the corner, I place my food on the table, take a seat and put my bag on the chair beside me.

The food is delicious, as it has been since we arrived. My mind is all over the place. The argument with Stacee has really got to me, to add to that, my emotions are like a rollercoaster. Everything Brooklyn said to me is also playing on my mind. I can feel the tears rearing to the surface, so I stand up, gather my bag, then leaving the dining room.

I go and find a sun lounger near the pool on the far side, that can't be seen from our room. I drop my bag at the side and sit down, that's when the tears begin the fall. The thought of losing something that I didn't know I wanted, makes my heart ache with loss. People are not meant to fall in love after a few days, it takes months, sometimes years to truly love someone. Yet here I am crying, because I'm falling in love with Brooklyn and I can't even be with him because we leave the day after tomorrow.

Also, I feel terrible for saying those things to Stacee. I should be happy for her that she's found someone but I can't, because I want to be with Brooklyn too. It's just an impossible situation. The tears fall even more, making my vision blurry.

"What's a beautiful girl like you sitting over here on her own?"

A voice says from behind me says, it's was Brooklyn. I quickly wipe my eyes but he walks from behind me and stands in front of me, he notices my tears and crouches down.

"Hey baby, what's wrong?"

I shake my head and cover my face.

"Taylor, baby. Do you want to talk about it?"

Again, I just shake my head.

"Come on babe, come up to my room, we can talk there all the lads are out."

He pulls me up by my hand and I grab my bag off the floor. We go up the small set of steps, and walk to the lift. We enter and press the button for the third floor. Arriving at that floor, we leave the lift, walk down the corridor, and then stop outside room four hundred. Brooklyn takes out his key card and unlocks the door and he motions for me to go in first. His room layout is different to mine and Stacee's. As I walk in there's a settee that looks to be a pull-out bed with pillow and blanket, in front of that there is a coffee table and a TV on a stand by the wall. I hear the door close and Brooklyn catches my hand, leading me through to one of three doors off to the side of the main room.

"Cameron sleeps out there, Leo and Nathan share that room." He says pointing to the room that has a closed door.

"That's the other bathroom and this is my room." He explains as he guides me further into the room. He closes the door and locks it.

"Just in case the guys come back, so we can talk in private."

I drop my bag on to the table in the corner, then go to sit on the bed.

"So, Taylor, do you want to tell me what's got you so upset tonight?"

I start to shake my head, when he walks toward me.

"It's stupid really, I got into it with Stacee, I said some nasty things to her and…"

"Start from the beginning, Taylor."

So, I go on to explain about Jake and how Stacee was trying to set me up and then I pause.

"So, she tried to set you up with this guy from the plane you were on together. Why didn't you want to go out and have a good time with this guy? I will admit though, I wouldn't want you to but if that's what you wanted."

I stand up and start pacing back and forth, Brooklyn stands as well and walks towards me.

"Taylor, do you feel the same way I do about you, about me?"

I just nod.

"Tell me how you feel Taylor, be honest please."

"Brooklyn, over the last week I have gotten to know you, you make me feel things that I have never felt before. My heart flutters when your near, my chest feels like it's going to explode. My body comes alive when we are together, the fire ignites inside me. You give me goose bumps when you kiss me. I want more but I'm afraid that you don't want it too. Earlier on while we were on that beach…"

I pause trying to think of the right way to explain it all.

I was aroused," he finishes for me.

"Yeah you were, but you also seemed distracted, like you were holding back. It felt like you wanted to take things further but something changed."

His hand comes up and cups my face.

"Taylor," he says, then his lips are on mine, his hunger for me matches mine.

I wrap my arms around his neck, run my hands up through the back of his hair and pull on it. My body is burning for more of his touch, I thought he would pull away at any moment, but he didn't. He picks me up and I wrap my legs around his waist. Walking us over to the bed our lips don't even separate and he moans into my mouth. Placing me onto the edge of bed, he stands up, then starts removing his shirt, dropping it to the floor. His chest is perfectly toned, you can tell he spends time working out. I run my hands up over his chest and lean forward so I can kiss his stomach and make my way up his chest.

Brooklyn breath is laboured, he's appears as turned on as much as I am. Slowly I ease myself off the bed and stand in front of him. I move the straps of my dress down my shoulders, letting them fall down my arms and the dress falls to the floor. Twisting my arms behind me, I undo my bra and let it fall to my feet.

"Taylor, you are so beautiful."

I reach out, grab the waistband of his shorts, undo the button, and slowly ease the zip down, as they fall, I notice he's commando. His hard length is poking up and he hisses as my hand brushes against his dick as pull down his shorts. He steps out of them, and kicks them away. He just stands there naked, as his thick massive dick points up, he then leans forward and kisses me on the lips. His hands move towards my waist and his fingers do to the elastic of my knickers and slowly removes them. As he does, he kisses down my chest, stopping at my breasts. His tongue comes out and he flicks my nipple, then sucks on it hard and lets it go. He moves on to my other one and repeats the action. He kisses down my body, while easing my knickers down my legs, to the floor, where I step out of them. Dropping to his knees, he's level with the apex of my thighs. Giving me a gentle push, I fall onto my back on the bed and his hands slowly spread my legs.

My shaven pussy is on full display, there's no room for modesty. He crawls closer to me and lowers his mouth on my pussy placing soft, long licks, while he pushes two fingers inside of me. The feeling is so intense, that I feel like I'm about to blow. He sucks harder, while his fingers continue their assault, it's then an intense pressure forms in me.

"Oh my God, I'm going to... Oh fuck...." I scream and my hands grip the blanket, as an orgasm explodes from me.

I'm panting so hard; I've never had an orgasm so stimulating as that before. Brooklyn crawls onto the bed, kissing his way up to my face, where he hovers over me, gazing into my eyes.

"Wow Brooklyn, your mouth and tongue have hidden talents," I say in between painting.

"You have no idea baby," he says as he kisses me.

I can taste myself on his lips and tongue. He slowly lowers himself and enters me, omg he's massive. He pauses for a second allowing me to adjust to his huge dick, then he pushes forward, entering me fully.

We spend the rest of the night tangled in each other's arms, exploring each other's bodies until the sun comes up.

Chapter Thirteen

'*Bang,* bang.'

Someone banging on the door wakes me up, I jump up and glance around and I suddenly remember that I am not in my room, I'm in Brooklyn's.

"Morning beautiful," he says gazing at me from his pillow.

There is another bang on the door.

"Brooklyn, you in there? We are heading down to breakfast. Are you coming?" Cameron says from the other side of the door.

"I'm busy, I'll come down a little while." he shouts, then reaches for me and pulls me against his chest.

"Taylor are you regretting last night?" he whispers.

"No, but I am gutted this is our last day together before we fly home tomorrow. Just when we finally get together, I have to say goodbye. It's just not fair." I say as tears begin to fall.

He pulls me closer, wrapping his arms tighter around me.

"We can try the long-distance thing; I can come visit you and you can come see me. Also, we can always use social media or video chat until we can meet again in person." he says, then kisses the top of my head.

"Yeah I suppose, if only we lived closer, this wouldn't be so hard." I say and close my eyes.

Once we prise ourselves from each other and out of the bed, we went for breakfast, then Brooklyn came back to my room with me, so I could change and so I wouldn't be alone with Stacee.

After our argument yesterday, I felt weird about going into the room alone. As I opened the door, silence greeted us, Stacee was gone, her suitcase was packed. There was a note, that said she was sorry about everything and that she had gone to say goodbye to Raph. I packed my suitcase and left out an outfit out for tonight and the flight home, as it would be colder once we reached Wales.

I spend the rest of the morning and afternoon, poolside with Brooklyn, we both didn't want to be apart. I know he said we could do the long-distance thing, talk on social media, and video chat, but it wouldn't be the same. My heart feels like it's being ripped out at the thought that in just a few hours it will be the end of us.

"There you are dude; I should've guessed you would be with Taylor. Leo and Nathan are playing pool in the bar with some chicks. I was on my way back when I spotted you by the pool." Cameron says as he sits on the empty sun lounger beside me.

"So, Taylor you off home tomorrow?" He asks.

"Yeah we are, I wish we weren't though, but all good things must come to an end at some point, right."

"Yeah very true. You should join us in the downstairs bar for a few games of pool and watch the show Tina T, she's supposed to be really good."

I agree to go with them as it's our last night here but I had to make things right with Stacee first. Brooklyn goes with Cameron as I made my way back up to the room to have a chat with Stacee. I open the door and she is sat on the bed and glances up as I walk into the room.

"T, I'm so sorry I've been acting like a real bitch the last few days. I don't want this argument to ruin our holiday. We came here together for a week of celebration and we haven't really spend much time together." She says as she climbs up off the bed and walks over to me.

"Stacee I'm sorry too I was a nasty bitch and you didn't deserve what I said to you, will you forgive me?" I beg.

She wraps her arms around me.

"Of course I forgive you, will you forgive me?" she asks and I nod.

"Yes, let's forget it happened."

I tell her about Cameron's invite for this evening and about what happened with Brooklyn.

Chapter Fourteen

The downstairs bar is quiet, Brooklyn and his friends are standing around the pool table. Suzy is sat on a stool by the bar and Brie is leaning over the pool table. I haven't really spoken to them since the time at beach when I pissed Brie off, I pause and turn to Stacee.

"I need you to come to the ladies with me," I say, then grab her and pull her towards the toilets.

"Jesus T, what's up with you? You were really excited and basically pushed me out the door to get down here so fast." She says as I lean my back against the sink.

"Okay, so remember when I left you in bed and went to the beach with the two girls next door?"

She nods.

"Well Brie, one of the girls said she fancied the lad that she had seen on the beach previously. Well he turned up, whilst we were together and she pointed him out to me. He had been in the water and was walking towards us." I pause.

"So, what happened?" She asks encouraging me to tell her the rest.

"That lad was Brooklyn. He walked up to us, held out his hand and pulled me to my feet, then started kissing me in front of everyone, including Brie."

"Oh wow."

"Yeah, you could say that, she pretty much stormed off. She was really pissed off from what her sister was saying, as she had been trying to grab his attention from the moment, she laid eyes on him. I didn't see her when she came back because Brooklyn took me for a walk. Now, she's in that room playing pool with Brooklyn and his friends."

"T, you will be fine, don't worry I got your back if she starts…."

"Taylor has nothing to worry about, Brie hooked up with Leo the other night. Even if she did, Brooklyn is in love with you, no other woman is even on his radar." Suzy says from the doorway.

I don't know how long she had been stood there, but it was as if she could read my mind.

"I noticed you both walk from the bar to here, I wanted to follow you in case you were worried about being in the same room as Brie. She is too busy flirting with Leo to notice anyone else," she smiles.

"Hey, we haven't been introduced, I'm Stacee, Taylor's friend," Stacee says while shaking Suzy hand.

"I'm Suzy, are you girls going to come back in and join me by the bar?"

"Yeah, let's go grab a seat before it starts to get busy." I say to them both.

We leave the toilets and walk across to the bar. As the three of us walk in, we notice that we are being watched. We stroll over to the bar, order some cocktails and take a seat on the bar stools. Brooklyn hands his cue to Nathan, then stalks his way over to me. Before I have a chance to speak, he cups my face and places a dominating kiss on my mouth. Cat calls from his friends sound in the background and we break apart, leaving me gasping for air.

"You look stunning in that dress; your long legs look good enough to taste…"

"Hey lover boy, put the girl down for a minute, we have a game to finish." Nathan says to him, pointing his pool cue towards him.

"I don't want to play anymore." Brooklyn replies.

"No way, you're my doubles partner, you have to play…"

"Nathan is right, go finish playing, I'll be here by the bar when you are done." I tell him and give him a little shove and a smile.

He reluctantly goes back to the pool table to take his shot.

"Bloody hell T, that was intense, he is bat shit crazy about you. I can see it now, you would make an awesome couple, the sexual tension oozes from you both."

"I agree with Stacee, you could cut the air around you with a knife ." Suzy adds.

Brie walks towards up to the bar and orders a drink. I straighten up on my stool, ready for whatever she's going to say.

"Listen Taylor about the other day, I just want to say sorry for storming off. I don't take losing to others well and I shouldn't have acted like I did. It's plain to see he only has eyes for you. Can we forget it happened?" Brie asks and I agree.

Once the game the lads and Brie were playing was done, we all went to play a game, Stacee and Brie, verses me and Suzy. Stacee was kind of kicking our arses and then Suzy had a fluke shot and potted all the balls. We played the best of five games and by the end of the fifth game, tonight's entertainment was starting to set up. More people were coming into the bar, so we grabbed a table while we could.

The singer was brilliant, her voice was very powerful and easy to listen to, she would knock spots off most of the singers and bands I've come across. Leo pulls Brie up to dance a few other people join them on the dance floor. The song changes, she start singing, Rewrite The Stars, from The Greatest Showman.

"Come dance with me?" Brooklyn asks and holds his hand out, I take it and pass my bag to Stacee, who is talking to Suzy.

He leads me on to the dancefloor and starts to twirl me out and back to him. One hand holds my waist, while his other catches my hand, and he starts singing along to the song. Dropping both hands to my waist, he pulls me closer; I wrap my arms around his neck and lean my head on his shoulder. The song changes to a cover of Olly Murs,

Moves, and everyone else joins us on the dance floor. Stacee dances over to us and passes me my bag, then joins Suzy and Nathan.

We spend the next hour dancing, the music is blasting and everyone dances to the music. Brooklyn leans into to whisper something in my ear.

"Come and get a drink with me in the upstairs bar, then we can go back to my room."

I nod in agreement and we weave our way through all the bodies on the dance floor and leave the bar. We walk up the steps and go to the bar in the lobby. It's quiet up here, probably because everyone was downstairs enjoying the entertainment. We order two cocktails and head up to his room. Opening the door, Brooklyn holds it open for me to go in first, then he follows, closing the door behind him. We go into his room and he places his drink on the table in the corner, before closing and locking his bedroom door. He walks over to the curtains, just to the side of the bed and opens them, revealing a set of doors, leading to a balcony and opens them.

"Wow, your room is so much better than ours, we only have the one balcony, that overlooks the main swimming pool."

I place my drink beside his, then start digging through my bag to find my phone. Unlocking the screen, I send a quick text to Stacee, so she knows where I am, pick up my drink and walk out onto the balcony. Brooklyn goes back inside to grab his drink, then joins me on the balcony.

"Are you all packed, ready for flying home tomorrow?"

"Yeah, I am, I did mine earlier. I can't believe this is our last night."

"Give me your drink."

So I pass it to him and he places them on the patio table in the corner.

"Where is your phone?" he asks.

I unlock it and hand it to him. He swipes across to the camera.

"Come here."

He turns his back so it's against the wall of the balcony and holds me under one arm, then takes a selfie.

"Let's take some more photos together," he suggests then pulls me back into the hotel room.

Brooklyn flicks on the light, sits on the bed and motions for me to join him. I kick off my sandals and join him, he snaps a few pics of us making funny faces and some normal pictures. We move up the bed and lean against the headboard, I scroll through my photo gallery on my phone. We laugh at all the silly ones with the funny faces. As I scroll across, I come to the photo of me and Jake.

"Who's that?" He asks pointing at the screen.

"Oh, that's just Jake, the lad Stacee tried to set me up with."

Brooklyn's body language suddenly changes, he takes my phone out of my hand and places it on the bedside table, at his side of the bed. Then he's on me lightning, kissing me, then his hands move under my dress, reaching for the apex of my thighs.

"God Taylor, your soaked, stand up," he orders.

Climbing off me, he stands up and pulls the curtains closed. Stripping out of his clothes, I notice his cock is hard and pointing north. I slowly pull my dress down my body; my breasts bounce free. I never wear a bra with this dress, as it's visible at back. My knickers are wet, as I ease them down my legs. Brooklyn stalks towards me, catching my hand, he moves backwards, then let's go of my hand. He lays on his back on the bed.

Come here Taylor," he orders.

I crawl up the bed and hover over him, with my knees on the bed. Brooklyn uses his hand to line his cock up with my entrance and pushes me down. He hisses at the feeling of our bodies connecting, then cups my face and kisses me with such passion. My pussy feels so full with his massive cock inside me. I lean on his chest, sit up and start riding his cock, his hands squeeze my breasts, as I bounce up and down him. I can feel my orgasm building, My movements increase in speed until…

"Oh, my, god." I scream as I come hard.

Brooklyn flips me over, holding my legs above his shoulders, enters me and pounds into my pussy, it's not long before his moans fill the room. We both fall on to the bed panting and breathing heavily. It's gone quiet when I open my eyes and I notice that Brooklyn is sleeping. I slowly ease myself out of the bed and throw my dress back on. I don't know where my knickers ended up, so I don't bother looking for them. Instead I grab my phone, bag, sandals and tiptoe to the bedroom door, I ease it open and walk out into the main part of the room. Cameron glances up and smiles.

"Hey Taylor, have a good night with my boy

"I did, can you tell him I'll text him when he goes back home." I whisper.

"Sure, thing sweetheart, you love books, right?" He asks as I walk towards the door to leave.

"Yeah, why?"

"Oh, I heard there is some big author event in Cardiff, isn't that where you are from?"

"Yeah, I am, I've heard about that event, my friend bought us tickets a while ago when it was announced. It's called Romance and Villains Author Event; they have one every year. Thanks for telling me, I better go as we have an early flight." I reply before opening the door and leaving.

Chapter Fifteen

The plane ride back home to Wales was quiet. Stacee slept most of the way back, instead of Jake, some older lady sat beside us.

The buzz from the inside of the aircraft wasn't like it was flying over to Tenerife. It was quiet, cool, and calm, the complete opposite to what it was on the flight over. I had my eyes closed most of the time, I couldn't stop thinking about Brooklyn. About the time we spent together, exploring each other's bodies.

It felt like it took twice as long to reach Cardiff. When we landed, we flew through check-in, collected our suitcases, and made our way outside, to wait for a taxi. One arrived fairly quickly, so we got in, told the driver our address, and made the journey home.

Love
Five Weeks Later

It's finally Friday, work has been so crazy the last five weeks and time has flown by.

I haven't seen Stacee since we both started our teaching assistant jobs in different schools. I am so glad it's the weekend, I could really use a drink tonight to unwind. So I've agreed to meet Stacee at The Red Lion at seven, for a catch up.

The last bell indicating the end of school rings, all the kids pack their belongings away, then start rushing out the door. I press a few buttons on my laptop and begin to close it down, when my colleague Rob, taps the door.

"Hey Taylor, a few of us are going for a few drinks after work, if you fancy coming?" He asks as he walks up to my desk and leans against the side of it.

"Thanks, but I'm going home and then I'm off out with my friend, but thanks for asking." I reply smiling at him.

"Sure, maybe another time, have a good weekend." He says, then leaves.

Rob has been trying to get me to go out with him since I started at the school. I was telling Stacee on the phone the other night and she thinks he fancies me. I disagreed with her but now I'm starting to think she's right.

Packing my laptop in to my bag, along with the English homework I have to mark, I zip it up and pick up my empty mug. Making my way to the staff room, I drop my mug in the sink and grab my coat, then leave to go home.

Just as I open my front door, my phone starts ringing, its Stacee.

"Hello," I say kicking the door shut behind me.

"T, are you ready for some fun and to let your hair down? I swear I didn't realise how much hard work it was going to be working in primary school." She moans.

Laughing, I reply, "Stacee, you knew what you were signing up for when we started the course and where it would lead."

"Yeah, I know, but I swear it's only been what nearly five weeks and I already thinking of a career change. The kids are okay, it's the snotty nose teachers that are getting on my nerves to be honest. There is this one teacher, Mrs Jones, grrrr... she just pisses me off."

"Well, I'll swap you Mrs Jones for Rob. He asked me to go out with him and a few others again. I bet you any money, if I did say yes, it would only be just me and him. He would probably make some excuse for nobody else being there, he's constantly trying to flirt with me. I don't know what to do to make him to get the bloody message that I am not interested." I say, after I dump my bag on the sofa and sit down.

Stacee is in a fit of laughter on the other end of the phone.

"Stacee, this isn't funny, he's like a love sick puppy." I add causing her to laugh even louder.

"T, I don't see the problem, you're single and so is he. You should go on one date with him, just to keep him happy."

"I don't want a man in my life, I'm happy being young, free and single…"

"T, that is total bull and you know it, you are still hung up on your holiday fling. Have you heard from him since we got back?"

"I spoke to him on the phone when we arrived back home after the holiday, he's sent a few texts but he's been busy and so have I." I try to explain.

"T, forget about Brooklyn, we are going out tonight. I'm going to swing by yours at six-thirty and we are going into town to check out the new club Express. So make sure you wear your hottest outfit, because you need to get laid and forget about him, so be ready," she says, then hangs up without giving me a chance to reply.

I glance at the clock, it's nearly five, so I haven't got time to mark the English homework. Instead, I walk into the kitchen and plug my phone in to charge, then grab a microwavable curry from the freezer and pop it into the microwave.

I head upstairs to my bedroom and find something to wear in my wardrobe. I pick out my black mini, strappy dress and matching black heels and lay them on the bed, then strip out of my coat and work clothes. I pad across the landing to the bathroom naked, turn on the shower, wait a few minutes for it to heat up and climb in under the warm water. I begin washing away the long school day from my skin and hair. Once I'm done, I grab a towel and wrap it around my body, then grabbing a second one wrap it around my hair. Leaving the bathroom, I head downstairs and into the kitchen and over to the microwave. Opening it, I pull out my curry and give it a little shake, before putting it back in for another five minutes.

While I wait, I check my phone and go through my social media. There's nothing new, so I type Brooklyn's name in and his profile comes up. I notice that he's recently posted a photo of him and some girl in London.

I guess everything he said was a lie.

The microwave pings, so I retrieve my curry and place the container onto a plate, grab a fork and begin eating. Once I'm done, I clean up the kitchen, then head upstairs to get ready. I towel dry my body, then putt on my black bra and panties. After blow drying my hair, I and curl it like I use when in college. I start applying some foundation, lipstick, and eyeshadow. Lifting my dress off the hanger, I step into it and wiggle it up my body, putting my arms through the thin black straps. I slip on my black shoes and sit on the end of the bed to do up the straps. Standing back up, I straighten my dress out and walk over to my wardrobe, grab my black jacket, slip it on. and grab my black clutch purse from the bottom of my wardrobe.

Walking over to my long mirror in the corner, I check my reflection, my outfit looks perfect , if I say so myself. I go to my small white, dressing table and open the drawer to pull out my perfume and notice my sanitary towels.

"Shit." I say before rushing out the room, down the stairs and grab my phone, pulling up my calendar.

My period was late, it must be the stress.

I can't be pregnant.

My phone rings, making me jump.

"Hello."

"T, I'm five minutes away, wait outside and the taxi can drop us into town." Stacee says, then hangs up.

I quickly run back upstairs and grab my perfume, slamming the drawer shut, then run back downstairs. Picking up some cash, my ID, keys, perfume, and phone, I slip them inside my bag. Turning off the lights and closing the door, I go outside to wait for Stacee.

Love

The Express is packed, we are standing by the bar waiting for our drinks. I order a coke, as my heads all over the place. Seeing the pads in the drawer stunned me. I'm never normally late, I'm like clockwork every month.

"Stacee, I need to go home, okay. I'm sorry but I can't stay." I say, then turn and rush off towards the exit.

Following behind me, she shouts, "Hey T, slow down what's wrong? You're never normally this quiet, like you have been tonight."

I reach out, grab her hand and we go out the exit, pass the bouncers I let go of her hand and turn to her.

"I think I may have come back with something from the holiday."

"What are you on about T, you're not making any sense. Come on Taylor, you know you can tell me anything." She says and catches my arm, moving us around the corner from the club.

Taking a deep breath, I turn away from her briefly, then turn back to face her.

"Stacee my period is late."

She opens her mouth, then closes it. "Taylor, did you use any protection with Brooklyn?" She asks and I shake my head.

"How many times T, did you have sex with him unprotected?"

"I don't know, maybe eight times, the night before we left, he was so horny, he fucked me so many times so I can't be sure."

"Okay, in that case you need to do a test as soon as possible."

"I will tomorrow."

"Oh no, you're doing one tonight. We are going to Tesco, they don't shut until midnight and it's not even close to that, so come on." She says, then flags down a taxi, we jump in and he drops us at the local Tesco.

Walking to the aisle where the pregnancy tests are located, I grab a Clear Blue one and go to pay for it. Stacee pulls me towards to toilets and pushes the door open.

"You need to do the test tonight."

"I don't know if I can Stacee, I'm scared."

"T, just go in the toilet cubicle and piss on the stick. It will put your mind at ease. Either you are knocked up or your just late."

I hand her my bag, go into the cubicle, open the box, and unwrap the pregnancy stick. I pull my dress up and knickers down, then sit on the toilet, hold the stick between my legs and pee. Once I'm done, I put the other end cap on the test, pull my knickers up, straighten my dress and flush the toilet. Opening the door, Stacee hands me my bag, I place it on the counter and turn the test upside down and wash my hands.

"Stacee, I am so freaking nervous, how can I be so stupid? I haven't been taking my contraceptive pill for two months. I was meant to go see the doctor after I run out but I didn't." I say as the tears are building and my hands are shaking.

"Stacee, I can't do it; will you look please?" I ask her and she nods, then walks over counter and picks the test up.

"T, your pregnant." She says.

It's then the dam breaks, tears fall down hard my cheeks. She places the test inside my purse, then wraps her arms around me, letting me cry from the shock.

Love

It took a while for it all to sink in, but after I did the test in Tesco, I wanted to be sure, so I booked myself a doctor's appointment and they confirmed it. I'm meant to be going to an author event in Cardiff next month with Stacee. With the way I'm feeling with my hormones all over the place, I'm not sure I want to go. I haven't heard from Brooklyn since the last time I spoke to him. I haven't even bothered to stalk his profile on social media.

Stacee has been amazing though all of this. She's even moved out of her parents' house and in with me, into my spare room. The morning sickness started a few days ago and it's more like all-day sickness. I spend a lot of the time with my head down the toilet, throwing my guts up. Stacee did some research and found out that Strong mints help with it, so she got me a shed-load to help me and so far, they worked.

Chapter Sixteen

A Month Later

"Stacee, thank you for pushing me to come today. I've been really looking forward to this event for ages. Romance and Villains is the event all the bloggers and authors have been talking about all over social media." I say as I wheel my small box behind me with my books, blank canvas, and posters, I made for authors to sign, towards the venue.

"I know, plus, did you see the gorgeous cover models that are going to be at the event, Bruce Phillips, Ryan Leigh, also the new one in the modelling industry, Kyle Johnson. I am definitely getting photos with those guys." Stacee giggles as we approach the Plaza hotel.

"Girl, you are men crazy."

"Wow, the hotel was absolutely massive, look there is the queue. Did you print the tickets off before?" she asks as we join the other readers in the queue.

"Yeah I did." I reply and dig in to the front part of my bag and show her.

"T, have you heard anything from Brooklyn yet?" She asks as the line moves slowly towards the entrance of the hotel.

"No and to be honest, I doubt I will ever see or hear from him again. I'm going to forget about men and just focus on me and my bump. Men are off limits for a while. When bump is born, I will have my hands full and won't have time to date." I say just as we get to the front.

I hand the tickets over to the woman at the entrance table and she scans them. We walk into the hotel lobby, the door to the side of it, has a massive banner indicating which room the signing is in.

"Stacee, can we please not mention Brooklyn for the rest of the day please, I want to enjoy it without thinking about him." I say and she agrees.

We head into the room in search of the well-known authors that were listed on the event banner, including my favourite Michelle Valentine. As we approach her table there are five people in front of us, so I dig in my box on wheels, grab the poster and all the Black Falcon books of hers. I had bought them from Amazon before coming here. It's finally my turn.

"Hi Michelle, can you sign these please." I ask.

She smiles at me and starts to signs the books and poster, I made with her book covers on.

"How is your day going so far?" She asks.

"We haven't long arrived, I have been so excited for today, I have about fifteen pre-orders to pick up. I also pre-ordered the two Hard Knocks books of yours as well." I explain.

She asks her PA to have a look through the box of the floor for them, after locating them, she places the small, white bag with the two books on the table. Michelle hands me back the Black Falcon books, then takes the books out of the bag and signs them. Once she was done, she asks for a hug and I ask her to have a photo with her, to which she agrees. She is such an amazing author, one of my favourites, her southern accent is so sweet.

Once her PA has taken our photo with my phone, I say thank you, step to the side and wait for Stacee, as she pre ordered the same books as me. After she had her books signed and her photo with Michelle, we move around the room.

We meet a few authors we know and a lot of new authors too. Stacee spots two of the male models walking towards, author Jessica Parker's table. Kyle, the cover model for four of her books, has attended with her. On the table next to her is one of the models that Stacee fancies the pants off. So she makes a beeline for Jessica's table, not bothering to wait for me. I laugh at her behaviour, you would swear that Kyle was standing up with open arms for her to run to, the way she was acting. In reality, he is just sitting beside Jessica, signing books and calendars. As I approach the table I Stacee asks if she can have a couple of photos, one with both Jessica and one with just Kyle the on his own. Stacee hands me her phone and I take the photos for her; then we walk over to the table with the other male model and we do the same again.

While Stacee poses with Ryan, I glance around and notice a massive banner, that states Tenerife Temptation by B.J. Parker. Across the front, it states, *Advance copies available, releasing twentieth of September.* That's five days from now, I look back to see if Stacee was finished, that's when she walks towards me.

"Oh my God, he's so freaking hot. Did you see those muscles and his tattoos?"

"Yeah, kind of hard not to miss with his shirt off. Quick, let's jump in line for this author, B.J. Parker, he's got advanced copies of his next release."

I explain, then pull her along with me until we are standing in the line to see the author. As we reach the front of the line, B.J. has his head down and is currently signing books and a kindle cover. When it's my turn, I move to the front of the table.

"Hi, how are you girls? Are you enjoying yourselves today?" he ask, as he looks up from checking his phone and placing it back down on the table.

OMG, that voice, those eyes, it can't be… I can't speak, I can't, it's him… My chest feels really tight and I'm struggling for breath, it feels like I been punched. Stacee nudges me.

"I... umm." I stammer, still struggling to speak.

"She wants a copy of your book, Tenerife Temptation." Stacee explains.

I stand there in silence, shocked that I'm standing in front of Brooklyn again. He grabs a book from a box on the floor and signs it, then holds it out to me, but Stacee grabs it first and hands him some cash. I quickly turn around and rush towards the exit.

"T, slowdown will you, where you going?" Stacee shouts, causing a few heads to turn.

I pause once we are in the lobby.

"I can't believe its him Stacee, he here. He writes books, he never said he was an author." I rush out, panicked.

"Taylor, you need to calm down okay, I think he was in as much shocked to see you, as you were to see him. Calm down, stressing can't be good for the baby." She says as Brooklyn comes the door, with Cameron by his side and his eyes land on us.

"I need the toilet." I say, then run off, leaving all my belongings with Stacee.

It all makes sense now why Cameron mentioned the event when I was leaving Brooklyn's room that night. I thought it was weird, but now it makes sense. He knew Brooklyn would be attending the event, but failed to mention that fact. I'm sitting on the toilet with my head in my hands, when there is a knock on the cubicle door.

"T, are you in here, are you okay?" Stacee asks from the other side.

I stand up and open the door.

"Stacee, I can't see him, not now. You can't tell him either" I say, holding my hand over my flat stomach where my baby is growing.

"T, he's gone back inside, Cameron is waiting with our things. Brooklyn is here to do a job and sign books and meet fans. He noticed you run off the moment you saw him coming. So, he knows you don't want to talk right now. He does want to talk to you though. He has the author meal tonight but he wants to slip away to meet up with you, so he can explain things."

The damn breaks and the tears fall.

"I don't know if I can." I reply in between sobs.

"T, you need to hear what he has to say and maybe tell him about the baby. Come on, wash your face and we can leave if you want. I'll be with you, if you don't want to be alone with him."

I wash my face and dry it with some paper towels, then we make our way out of the toilet, back to the lobby, where Cameron was standing with our boxes.

"Taylor, I'm sorry you found out like you did. I wanted to say something but he's so damn secretive about this side of him. Only his brother knows he's an author and I only found out by accident. I didn't want you to get hurt like you have." He tries to explain, but Stacee cuts him off.

"To late jackass, thanks for watching our stuff, but you can go." She orders him, before grabbing both handles of our and wheels them away from him, leaving me stood in front of him.

"Thanks Cameron, a lot has happened since Tenerife, but I will meet him later. I pull an old receipt and pen out of my bag, then write my address on it, before handing it to him.

"Will you give this to him please?" I ask and he nods.

I walk off in the same direction Stacee went and found her waiting for me by entrance table.

"Let's go."

Tenerife Temptation

Chapter Seventeen

We haven't been home long. After the shock of seeing Brooklyn at the event, Stacee decided I needed to have some proper girl time. So she took me to a nail salon for some pampering and KFC for food.

"I'm going to jump in the shower, if he arrives and you don't want to be with him alone, just give me a shout okay?" Stacee says, then she's gone.

I start unpacking my books, Stacee had given me the book that Brooklyn had signed. I stand in silence, opening it up and find the message he left inside.

To the girl who stole my heart,
I'm so happy to see you again.
I hope you like happy ever afters.
A beautiful girl like you deserves her own
fairy-tale ending.

Love B.J. Parker

I close the book, take a deep breath, close my eyes, and opening them again, I continue unpacking my books. I place them on the tall, black bookcase by the side of my sofa. When I've finished, I make myself a hot chocolate and begin reading a pregnancy magazine that Stacee had bought me. As I'm reading an article on birth plans, there's a knock on the front door. Placing the magazine on the sofa beside me, I go to answer it. Pulling the door open, I notice Brooklyn and Cameron standing there.

"Hi, I guess you better come in."

They walk past me into the living room, closing the door behind them, I walk around them and sit on the sofa. Stacee walks in with a towel wrapped around her body.

"You can sit down if you want…"

"Actually T, Cameron can come with me into the kitchen, so you two can talk in private."

"Or maybe you can show me your bedroom." He replies with a wicked grin.

"Yeah in your dreams stud, you can go in the kitchen to wait, while I go get some clothes on," she says, pushing him towards the kitchen, then running upstairs.

Brooklyn walks over to the chair in the corner and sits down.

So…"

"So…" I reply, copying him.

He leans forward placing his arms on his thighs.

Tenerife Temptation

"Taylor, I am so sorry about you finding out like that, I never expected to see you again. Okay, that came out wrong, I mean I wanted to see you again, but because of the distance thing, I thought it wouldn't happen. I was shocked as you were to see you at the event…"

"Brooklyn, why didn't you tell me you were an author, instead of the story you give me in Tenerife."

"I was going to tell you but then I saw the photo of you and Jake, I wasn't sure if I could trust you…"

"What has a photo of me and some guy, I met on a plane have to do with this? I told you that I wasn't interested in him, so I really don't understand what your issue was. I wouldn't have told anyone your real name or …."

At that point Stacee sticks her head around the door.

"T, calm down you don't need to stress, okay and you stop stressing her out, it's not good for her," she says pointing at Brooklyn, before going back in the kitchen.

Brooklyn raises his eyebrows.

"Is she normally that protective?" he says, then stands up comes over to the sofa, picks up the magazine and puts it on the floor, then sits beside me.

"Taylor, the reason I had an issue with that photo is because that guy is my brother Jake..."

"What did you just say

"The guy in the photo, is my jackass brother Jake. He's the only one who knew I was an author. Cameron overheard a conversation me and Jake were having. Jake doesn't approve of me being an author because I write romance books, well more specifically, I am working on a few erotic romances. Tenerife Temptation was my first non-erotica book, it is dirty but it's more about a holiday romance, it's a two-part story."

Something he says about the book being a holiday romance bugs me.

"When did you start writing it?" I ask and he smiles.

"Well I started plotting it before the holiday, I wrote most of it while in Tenerife, on my tablet…"

"When did you finish it?"

He twists his hands together.

"I finished book one a week after we got home, then sent it to my editor and the cover designer. I wanted to have some advance copies for the event today."

"Do they get a happy ending?

"I'm not sure yet," he says, then stands up, walks over to the window, and gazes out onto the street.

"Brooklyn is the story about us?"

I notice his back rise and fall, as he breathes in and out heavily.

"Brooklyn."

He turns around, a sad look on his face.

"Yeah it is but I'm not sure how it's going to end… In the book, the leading male character makes this mistake and he doesn't realise it until it's too late to make it right."

I know what he is saying has double meaning. He's not just on about the characters in his book, he's on about himself. I stand up and walk over to where he's standing.

"Brooklyn, I want to forgive and forget the lies but how can I, when you haven't so much as text or called me in over three weeks. You've been posting photos of you and other women on social media, you've clearly moved on. I don't understand why you wanted to meet up with me."

My arms are crossed to stop myself from reaching out to him. My heart is saying, *forgive him* and my head is saying, *don't be an idiot think of the lies.*

"Taylor, that woman in the photos, is my sister, I mentioned her before. As for not texting, well things have been crazy. I go into my own little world when I'm writing and ignore everything and everyone around me. I know that makes it sound like a cop out and sound like a total ass but it's the truth…"

"He is telling you the truth Taylor; he's gone days without talking to me before now when he's in his writing cave…" Cameron pipes up from the kitchen

Stacee punches him in the chest, cutting him off.

"You idiot, you should have kept your mouth shut. You spoilt it, he should be on his hands and knees begging for forgiveness. You dumbass, you shouldn't have said anything to defend him, I'm sure he has a mouth of his own to speak." She says, hitting Cameron again.

"Stacee is right, Cameron shouldn't need to defend me, I can speak for myself. Taylor, I don't know what I have to do to make you forgive me for my actions, but I am so sorry I lied. I'm sorry I didn't tell you about Jake." He says as he walks over to where I am standing and catches my hand.

"Wait, what about Jake, how do you know him?" Stacee shouts, walking further into the room.

Brooklyn glances in her direction.

"The Jake you tried setting Taylor up with in Tenerife, is my brother."

"Oh shit, really?"

"Damn Stacee, you really tried to set Taylor up with that uptight prick, that was definitely the wrong brother to set her up with. My man Brooklyn is the guy for her." Cameron buts in, walks over to the sofa, picks up the magazine, and starts flicking through it.

"Wow, you would never have guessed you two were brothers, total opposites but you to have that charm about you." Stacee says.

"Thanks, I think." Brooklyn replies.

"When do you go back home?" I ask.

"We were going to go back tomorrow but…"

"So, which one of you girls is knocked up?" Cameron interrupts

I glance at Stacee and then at Brooklyn.

"That's our que to leave," Stacee quickly says and walks over to Cameron and pulls him by the hand up the stairs.

The sound of the door closing is the last noise before silence fills the house. I quickly walk away from Brooklyn and rush into the kitchen. I grab a glass from the cupboard and fill it with cold water from the tap. I take a few sips and close my eyes; this was not how I expected today to go. Brooklyn walks into the room and stops inches away from me.

"Taylor, are you pregnant?"

The tears I'd been holding back fall fast, his hand touches my back.

"Taylor turn around." He whispers.

I slowly start to turn and he takes the glass of water from my hand, placing it on the worktop and grabs my hand. I can't look at him, my eyes are blurred from crying. He let's go of my hands and wipes away my tears, then he cups my face.

"Taylor, are you pregnant?"

I can't speak, so I nod.

"Is it my baby?"

Again, I nod.

"I'm sorry, Brooklyn, I know you probably don't want kids but…"

He silences me with a kiss, before he pulls back.

"I want you; I want our baby. This child you are carrying was made from the love we have; we may not have realised it at the time but it was. You are mine and the precious gift inside you is also mine ,okay…"

He pauses and places a hand on my stomach where the baby is growing.

"We still have some stuff to talk about and more time to get to know each other, but I'm not walking away from you both. Not now, not ever."

Cupping the back of my head, he kisses me gently on the lips. This wasn't the reaction I was expecting, a lot of men would run a mile if a woman told them she was pregnant after a one- or two-night fling. Brooklyn has stunned me again; he just keeps on surprising me.

Chapter Eighteen

It's been a few weeks since Brooklyn accidentally found out I was pregnant, thanks to his friends big mouth. He had to go back to London to sort a few things out. He didn't want to go and it took a lot of persuading. Initially, he wanted to tell his family over the phone but with Stacee's help, we managed to persuade him to go and tell them in person.

Today is my second appointment with the midwife and I get to see the baby, while having a scan. I did tell Brooklyn yesterday that I was having first scan today, he was adamant that he would attend with me. He left London early this morning, to make sure that he was on time for the appointment. My starts ringing and I notice that its Brooklyn.

"Hello."

"Hey Taylor, I'm running late. I got caught in traffic, there has been a car crash on the M25."

"No worries, my appointment isn't until two forty-five, you have plenty of time," I say glancing at the clock on the wall.

"I promise I will try and get there soon, I better go, I'll see you in a little while," he says then hangs up.

Stacee is upstairs on the phone to Raphael, she told me he wants to visit for a catch up and have a night on the town. Or as I said to Stacee, *a night of being tied to the bed.*

I'm sitting on the sofa, watching Home and Away, with my bottle of water when there is a knock on the door Standing up, I go and answer it. Brooklyn is standing there wearing a white T-shirt and dark blue, denim Jeans, holding his keys in his hand.

"Are you ready to go?" He asks.

"Bugger, I lost track of time, I got to be at the hospital in twenty minutes I been trying to drink lots of water . I swear my bladder is ready to burst." I say and rush over to the sofa, picking the remote up and turning the TV off. I grab my bag, then rush back to the front door.

"Now I am."

We make our way to where his car is parked, jump in and I give him directions to the hospital,

When we arrive at St David's hospital, Brooklyn parks the car near the maternity entrance, we then head inside, so I can check in with the receptionist. We sit in the waiting area for about ten minutes before my name is called. I follow the nurse to a small room, that has a bed in the middle and a chair at the side. Walking over to the chair, I take a seat. The nurse asks me to stand on the scales to check my weight, then I step down go back to sit in the chair. She checks my blood pressure and then wraps a tourniquets around the top of my arm, so she can find a vein to take some blood from me. After she's done, I'm asked to go back out into the waiting room where Brooklyn is still sitting.

"Everything okay Taylor?" he asks as I sit on the chair beside him.

"Yeah, the nurse just checked my weight, blood pressure and took some bloods. I read in a pregnancy magazine that its normal." I tell him as I take the bottle of water out of my bag and drink half of it.

"I also read that for the sonographer to get a good scan picture, a woman should drink plenty water and have a full bladder." I explain, then drink the rest of the water.

Ten minutes later the female sonographer calls my name and I follow her into a small, dark room with a bed and a small computer with a black screen. Brooklyn follows me into the room, closing the door behind him.

"Can you confirm your name and date of birth for me please? Okay Taylor, if you would lay down on the bed and unbutton your trousers please." She says.

I do ask she asks, then she tucks a paper towel into the top of my trousers, then squirts some cold gel on to my stomach. Grabbing the doppler, she rubs it over my stomach, clicks a few buttons on the keyboard and pushes down on my stomach. The more she pushes, the more it makes me want to pee really badly. The sonographer presses a few more buttons then turns the computer screen towards me.

"There you go, that's your baby." She says as a beating sound fills the room.

"What is that sound?" Brooklyn asks her.

"That's the baby's heartbeat." She replies.

I stare at the computer screen, with my baby on it in amazement. My eyes begin to water and tears fall, but I'm not sad, I'm so happy. Brooklyn catches my hand, giving it a little squeeze. I'm lost for words; I've never felt love for another person like I do for the baby inside me. Seeing the baby makes it all feel so real. Some part of me felt like it wasn't real, despite the positive test and morning sickness.

"Would you like a picture?" The sonographer asks me.

"Yes please." I reply, without talking my eyes off the screen.

"Okay, I'm going to take a few measurements of baby, then I will print some images for you to take home. There is a cost of one pound fifty, and you can pay at reception where you checked in."

After a few minutes she is done, she grabs another paper towel and wipes my stomach. Brooklyn let's go of my hand, so I button my trousers up. She hands me the scan photos in a small brown envelope.

"Thanks," I say as I stand up and Brooklyn opens the door for me and we walk out.

"I need the toilet before we leave."

"I'll go pay for the scan photos; you go to the toilet."

I was going to argue that I would pay but he walks off. Once I've taken care of business, I make my way back to reception where Brooklyn is sitting on a chair, waiting for me.

Standing up he says, "Ready to go?"

I nod and we make our way out of the hospital, back to his car, he unlocks it and we climb in. He puts the key into the ignition but doesn't start the car, instead he turns slightly in his seat to face me.

"Taylor, seeing our baby on the screen was just amazing, I can't believe how lucky I am. If I hadn't of met you in Tenerife, things would've have been so different for me."

He pauses, leans over and catches my hand.

"Meeting you has been the best thing to ever happen to me, I know that sounds cheesy but it's true. When I first laid eyes on you from across the pool, you took my breath away. You weren't like the other girls; you had your head in the book and had this energy about you. I don't know if anyone else could feel it but I could. Then when I spoke to you in the lobby for the first time, I felt something that I haven't felt for a long time. I know people say there is no such thing as love at first sight but Taylor, I fell in love with you at that moment. I'm crazy about you. I know I have been a total ass and my actions since Tenerife have been somewhat different to what I am saying. I love you so damn much. Seeing the life, we have created on that computer screen, makes me love you even more, if it's possible. I can't wait to be a dad and become a family. I have decided that I want to buy a house down here with you. I don't want to be a part-time father. Will you move in with me Taylor?"

I don't know if it's the hormones but I'm crying like a baby at his words.

"I… I don't know what to say." I stammer in between sobs.

"Taylor, I want us to bring our baby up together. I know it's too early for marriage. Hell, we are doing things backwards but I don't care. I want you and our baby with me and if that makes me sound like a sap, then fuck it, that's what I am. What do you say Taylor, will you move in with me?" He asks again.

"Brooklyn, you're an amazing guy and you surprise me all the time. A lot of men wouldn't want to stick around after a holiday fling…"

He tries to interrupt me, but I shake my head and hold my other hand up.

"But you want it all and now you want us to move in together. I am crazy about you as well; you were all I could think about since I've come home. Yes, I would love to move in with you. I love you so much, you are giving me a family."

He drops my hand, leans over, then cups my face with both hands.

"One day soon, I'm going to put a ring on your finger and marry you. I love you baby." He says, then kisses me on the lips.

Chapter Nineteen

Three Years Later

I roll over in bed and reach out to cuddle into Brooklyn but the space where he normally sleeps is empty. Opening my eyes, I glance at the clock, it's just after six in the morning. Flipping back the duvet cover, I climb out of bed and open the bedroom door. I can hear voices coming from downstairs. I walk across the landing, then tiptoe down the stairs towards the voices and pause at the bottom.

"Daddy, I'm super happy." My daughter says to her father.

"Why is that princess?"

"I'm a big girl daddy, I start school today." Our bubbly, three-year-old replies to him.

I step off the bottom step, where I was eavesdropping and walk into the room Brooklyn is sitting on the sofa, shirtless with Skylee sat on his lap. When she sees me, she jumps off, runs over to me and I pick her up.

"Skylee James, what are you doing up so early baby?"

"Mammy, I'm a big girl and I start school today," she replies, rather excitedly.

I laugh as I walk over to the sofa and sit beside Brooklyn.

"Sweetie, school doesn't start until nine o'clock, you don't need to be up this early, you should still be in bed sleeping."

"Skylee, why don't you watch some cartoons on the sofa, while me and daddy go make some breakfast." I

"Okay mammy." she says as she climbs off my lap.

I kiss her on the top of her head, stand up, grab Brooklyn's hand, and pull him up to his feet. We walk into the kitchen, where I let go of his hand, grab a small bowl from the cupboard and coco pops from the other. Pouring some in, I add the milk. Brooklyn picks up the bowl, grabs a spoon from the drawer and takes it into the living room for our daughter.

I flick the kettle on, grab two cups from the cup holder and place them in front of the kettle. I close my eyes for a moment and Brooklyn startles me by wrapping his arms around me from behind. He begins kissing my neck, then he pulls me back against him.

"You still manage to take my breath away baby, I love you so much. God help when our daughter starts dating, if she's anything like you, she will have lads falling at her feet. I'm going to have to have a baseball bat ready to beat them away." He chuckles against my neck, making my skin breakout in goose bumps.

I turn around in his arms, and wrap mine around his neck.

"We are both lucky to have you. You have been so amazing over the last few years, you still surprise me every day. Brooklyn, you have been so amazing with Skylee from the moment she was born. You got up with me for every night feed and nappy change. She really has got the best father in the world. I love you for everything you do for us" I say, then kiss him.

"Mammy, don't eat daddy face." Our daughter says interrupting us as she stands in the doorway holding her bowl.

We break apart, both laughing and I turn to face our daughter.

"Baby I wasn't eating daddy's face I was kissing him." I explain as I walk over to her and take her bowl from her.

She makes a funny face, before going back in the living room. Brooklyn is still laughing when I turn back around.

"That girl, she makes me laugh" he says before following Skylee.

I can hear him telling her to go play in her room for an hour, before she has to start getting ready for school, while he has a shower. I finish making the tea, then carry the cups upstairs into our bedroom and place them on the dresser. I can hear the shower running, so I poke my head into our daughters room to check on her. She's sitting on her bed, playing on her iPad.

Tenerife Temptation

I quietly close her door, walk to the bathroom, open the door slowly, walk in and lock it behind me. I pull my night dress over my head and drop my knickers to the floor. Climbing into the shower, I wrap my arms around Brooklyn. He turns around and cups my face, then kisses me hard.

"Someone is glad I joined them him the shower." I say pulling back a little, so I can speak.

"Baby, my cock has been like brick the moment you touch me." He replies hungrily.

"Then fuck me, take me now and make sure I can't walk properly for the rest of the day."

He lifts me up and holds me against the cold bathroom titles, then drives his thick, hard cock into my pussy, pounding into me as his lips devour mine. It's quick, hard, and fast. Ever since Skylee was born, when we've wanted some alone time, we do it when she's sleeping or playing.

Love

We drop Skylee off for her first day in school. She

was so excited, she didn't look back, just run off into class with all the other kids. We walk hand in hand out of the playground and back to the car.

Brooklyn is quiet as he's driving, I have a doctor's appointment this morning. I haven't told him yet; he thinks I have a dentist appointment as they are in the same building. So, as I haven't got work until later, Brooklyn said he would drop me off, he has a meeting in town anyway

"You're quiet Brooklyn, is everything okay?"

He quickly glances at me, then back to the road.

"Sorry yeah, I'm just thinking about this meeting. Remember the book I wrote Tenerife Temptation?"

"Yeah, the two-part holiday romance."

"Well this meeting is about that book. Just after Skylee was born, I had it turned into a script and I sent it off to a few producers. Well, two go back to me and they want to make it into a film. I'm meeting with them both to hear their thoughts and pitches, before I decide who to go with and sign any contracts."

"Wow, that is amazing. How come it's only now you are mentioning it?"

"I've kind of been putting it off, I didn't know what to do as the book was based on us, so it was special to me you know."

"Brooklyn, I wouldn't have minded; I love those books and I am so proud of you." I tell him and give his leg a little squeeze.

"Thank you, baby."

We pull up to the doctors, stopping by the entrance, I unbuckle my seatbelt, then lean over to kiss Brooklyn

"Good luck with the meeting." I say as I open my door, climb out and close it behind me.

Tenerife Temptation

He drives off and I head inside for my doctor's appointment, the waiting room is busy today.

A few days ago, I did a home pregnancy test. I was so nervous and I haven't told anyone yet. Instead, I made an appointment and here I am waiting to see if the test was right. I wanted to make sure I was hundred percent right, before I mentioned it to Brooklyn. I love him and he treats me like his queen. Skylee was a result of a holiday fling, I don't regret it one bit and neither does Brooklyn. He's told me he would love more kids, but wish we did things differently.

"Taylor Jones to room eight, with Doctor Kennedy," the voice over the tannoy says. I stand up and make my way to the doctors room.

Once I'm finished with the doctor and she confirmed my pregnancy, I walk out of the surgery and wait for a bus to go to town. While I wait, I send Brooklyn a text.

Hope the meeting is going well. Meet me back home at lunchtime, I'll cook us some lunch.

Then I hit send, my phone beeps just as the bus turns up. I climb on, pay the driver, and take a seat, then check my phone.

See you then baby. We can pick up where we left off x

He replies with a wink. As I'm not in work until after lunch, I grab a few bits in town and head home.

Love

I've just finished putting the finishing touches to the salad to go with the chicken breast, when the front door opens.

"I'm in the kitchen" I shout.

I pull the chicken from the oven, place it on the plates with the salad and new potatoes.

"Something smells lovely in here." Brooklyn says as he walks in.

He wraps his hands around me from behind, then kisses me on the cheek.

"It's only chicken with a salad and new potatoes, grab a seat."

He let's go of me, grabs some cutlery from the drawer and sits at the kitchen table. Picking up the plates, I walk over and place them on the table, then join him.

"How did the meeting go?"

He chews some of his food, before he replies.

"I signed the contract baby; they are making Tenerife Temptation into a film. The first guy I met was interested but I signed with the second guy I met up with, Martin. They are looking at doing casting as soon as next week and hoping to start shooting the film at the end of the year. As

I'm the author, I have say in who they cast in the leading roles too."

"That is amazing news Brooklyn, do you have any idea who they want to cast for the film?" I ask in between mouthfuls of my food.

"Not yet but I can't wait to see my books come alive and be up on the big screen. It's been a dream of mine for such a long time to have something that I have written made into a film or a TV adaptation. Now it's finally happening," he says beaming with happiness.

"I'm so proud of you, I know everyone will love the film as much as the books."

I finish my chicken and some of my potatoes, then go to the toilet. I glaze at my reflection in the bathroom mirror and grab the pregnancy test that's hidden in the back of the cupboard under the sink. I open the door and find rose petals on the floor outside the bathroom leading to our bedroom.

"B…"

I go to call Brooklyn but pause and follow the path petals Reaching the bedroom, I notice on the floor is a heart made from petals. Brooklyn is on one knee, holding a small black box up with the most gorgeous diamond ring.

"Taylor, I love you so much, you are my queen, my soulmate and the mother of my little princess. I fell head over heels for you from the moment I laid eyes on you. You make me feel alive when we are together. I feel lost when we are apart. Will you do me the honour of becoming my wife. Taylor Jones will you marry me?"

My heart is melting, tears of joy fill my eyes as I nod my acceptance. I drop the pregnancy test and cover my mouth with shock.

"Y... yes."

Brooklyn jumps up, takes the ring out of the box and places it on my ring finger. After kissing me on the lips, he glances down at the white stick on the floor and bends down to pick it up. He turns it over and his eyes widen.

"I was going to tell you, the doctor confirmed it today." I rush out.

"You're pregnant?" He asks and I nod.

"Hell yes, I'm going to be a dad again," he says then throws the test on the bed, picks me up, laying me on the bed and crawls up my body and peppers kisses all of me.

"Thank you, baby, you have given me everything. It's all thanks to you that my dreams have become a reality." he says while pushing up on to his elbows.

"So, you aren't mad we are having another baby?"

"Fuck no, I am on cloud nine baby. I love you Taylor, now get naked so I can show you how much," he orders.

Meeting Brooklyn has been the best thing to happen to me. If I hadn't of met him in Tenerife, my, life would've been so different. We wouldn't have our little princess. Tenerife Temptation, wouldn't have been written.

I wouldn't change any of it. Stacee on the other hand tried the long-distance thing with Raph, it was going well for a while but for her the holiday romance didn't last. She is now dating someone else that she met on a night out.

The End

L.M. Evans

Tenerife Temptation

Author Bio

L.M Evans is a stay at home mother who lives in South Wales with her husband and three children. She enjoys going for long walks in the countryside with her family and going to the movies.

When she's not busy running around after her children, you'll either find her working on her blog, writing. Or reading one of her favourite books.

In 2011 after a friend told her she should write her own book. She decided to write her first book called Ryder James. She published it in December 2014 and never looked back. Ryder James has since been revamped and is now under the new title Starstruck.

Tenerife Temptation

Contact Author

Facebook
https://www.facebook.com/AUTHORL.MEVANS/

Twitter
https://twitter.com/Louisem07021983?s=09

Instagram
Louisem070283

Blog Facebook Page ~
https://www.facebook.com/BLOGLMEVANS

Blog ~
https://louisemarieevans.blogspot.co.uk/?m=1&zx=50bb660e29 3dfa01

L.M. Evans

Printed in Great Britain
by Amazon